Published by Michael Terence Publishing, 2021

ISBN 9781800941267

Paperback and Amazon Kindle eBook editions

Working Again

Geoff Lambton

Michael Terence
Publishing

First published in paperback by
Michael Terence Publishing in 2022
www.mtp.agency

ISBN 9781800943612

Prologue

Part 1

Six Years Ago

'Twice as many people are killed by vending machines every year than are killed by sharks.'

The man driving the car remembered hearing those same words before. It must have been more than twenty years ago, but he never forgot it, mainly because he'd been working with vending machines for many years and had witnessed a lot of strange behaviour in people who came into contact with them. He even remembered the statistics. On that occasion the radio programme, which was all about sharks not vending machines, had informed him that four people were killed by sharks that year, which was one fewer than the average, meaning there are an average of ten people killed by vending machines every year. This didn't surprise him. He knew vending machines contained a strange power. They had the ability to induce irrational behaviour in people who used them or worked on them. His mate Liam was a prime example of this. He was amazed Liam hadn't electrocuted himself yet. There was a good chance he still might one day. Liam never saw the point of pulling the plug from the mains socket before poking around among a collection of wires which were used for conducting electricity.

Despite this, he had never witnessed anyone been killed by one, and had only heard of two deaths, both in the USA. One of those was when a machine was being lifted into a building with a crane but had slipped loose and landed on someone in the street below. The other one was something he could well believe happening, given some of the people he had encountered during his working life. A customer had been trying to buy a bar of chocolate which had unfortunately got stuck mid vend and the frustrated customer tried to retrieve it, but only succeeded in tipping the vending machine over and was crushed to death. He figured Americans were more likely to go to desperate measures to obtain the chocolate bar or crisps that they had paid for. British people would be more inclined to get revenge on the machine by beating the hell out of it and causing hundreds of pounds worth of damage because they were robbed of a bar of chocolate worth 80p.

Then the radio announced that there were seven people killed by sharks in the previous year. Two of those were a husband and wife from Australia. Being an England cricket fan, Australians were his natural enemy. He'd met quite a few of them over the years, mainly at cricket matches and in London pubs. He used to tell them they were well-balanced people. This was mainly due to the chip on each shoulder. He'd met some arrogant ones and some nice ones. The arrogant ones he tended to get on with reasonably well as they liked a good argument. He didn't like the nice ones so much. But he wouldn't wish getting chewed up by sharks on anyone. Or being squashed by a vending machine either.

Then the radio informed him that this particular Australian couple were killed while surfing in a place called Shark Bay. He paused for a moment to take the information in. Then as he often did, usually during a political debate, or a football commentary, he shouted and swore at the radio, which resulted in him not paying enough attention to the road and getting hooted at by other drivers.

'What the hell is wrong with you people? What do you expect to happen in a place called Shark Bay? There's a clue in the name. Why do you think it's called Shark Bay? It's not because it's full of fucking haddock!'

He was already convinced that human beings were the stupidest species on the planet. This pair from down under did little to change his mind. He pictured the scene on the morning of their last day alive.

'G'day Sheila. What shall we do today? How about a spot of canoeing up at Crocodile Creek?'

'Nah mate, I'm going to have to give that one a miss. I'm not gonna be doing any canoeing for a while. My arm's still a bit crook from last week.'

'It's your own fault. I told you not to stroke that funnel-web spider.'

'I know. But it looked so cute. And that's not why my arm is sore. I got stung.'

'Where did you get stung?'

'On my arm. I just told you.'

'Nah, you dingo. I meant where were you when it happened?'

'I went for a swim down at Jellyfish Lagoon. That was a bit of bad luck.'

'Yeah. Strewth. Who could have seen that coming?'

'Well, how about surfing then? I hear there's some big bonza waves up at Shark Bay.'

'Sounds terrific. I'll pack the hamper with some tucker and afterwards we could go for a picnic in Axe Murderer Wood.'

He wasn't the sort who suffered fools gladly, and these two must have been fools of the highest quality. The fantasy played out in his very peculiar mind, and reached the point when they had arrived at Shark Bay.

'C'mon in Sheila. The water's lovely.'

'Here I come. You're right. The water is lovely. And just look at the size of those waves. Bruce, I was just wondering. Shark Bay. It's an unusual name. Why do you think it's called… wait a minute. Can you hear something?'

'No. I can't hear anything.'

'Listen carefully. There it is again.'

'Oh Yeah. Some kind of musical instrument. Maybe a double bass? Sounds like durrrr dur.'

'Yeah, that's it. I can hear it too. Durrrr dur. Duuur dur. Dum dum dum dum dum dum dum dum.'

'It's probably nothing important. Anyway, you were saying?'

'Yeah. I was saying. Shark Bay. Why do you think it's… Ouch! Ah. That could be why.

He was snapped out of his fantasy when another driver hooted his horn at him. Unjustified he thought. The light had only just turned to green. You aren't supposed to move when it changes to amber. Amber means stop. It was drizzling and the sky was grey. He hated driving in conditions like this, mainly because people were too stupid or inconsiderate to put their lights on. How difficult would it be to just flick that little switch? On the best of days, he wasn't at all tolerant to the selfish behaviour of his fellow human beings. When he was in this mood, he would happily have an anti-tank missile system fitted to his car and blast all these bastards out of his way.

Cecil Barnard, or "Barney" as all his friends and work colleagues called him, turned off the radio. He had arrived at his destination. His mission was to repair one of the aforementioned killing machines. This was his job, which he'd been doing for many years. Today he was in one of those moods where he questioned why he was still doing it. He'd been out for a bit of a drink the previous evening and had a bad hangover, which didn't help, and it was cold and windy, with a bit of light rain thrown in. While most people would have preferred a dry and sunny day, Barney was happy with the cold and rain. It was the best weather for a hangover, as it brought everybody else down to his mood level. Also, the cold water splashing on his head was soothing. Whatever the weather, it was one of those days he would have been happier not getting out of bed. To make matters worse, his phone burst into life, and the name Grumbling Bowels flashed up.

Richard Bowles wasn't the worst manager he'd ever had, but was difficult to deal with when he was in one of his 'the customer is always right' moods. He'd been in that mood yesterday when Barney had been sent to get an irate customer's coffee machine working and found they had just forgotten to switch it on. The customer wouldn't accept any blame for this and insisted Barney gave them a detailed written report why the machine wasn't working. He duly obliged. His report read 'ON/OFF switch is ON OFF. ON/OFF switch should be ON ON. Switched ON/OFF switch from OFF to ON. Machine came ON.' This hadn't pleased the customer, or Bowles when they called him to complain.

Now he was calling again.

'Good morning Cecil.'

This got the conversation off to a bad start. He hated being called Cecil. Bowles knew that. And Barney knew that Bowles knew that. And Bowles knew that Barney knew that Bowles knew that.

'Good morning oh mighty leader. How can I help you?'

'I have just received the monthly report from the stores. You have used by far the most spare parts. Way more than all the other engineers.'

'That's alright. I aim to please.'

'You're missing the point. I'm not thanking you. Spare parts are very expensive. We can't afford to keep using this many parts.'

'I can easily solve that. I'll just do less work.'

'No. That is not an option.'

'Alternatively, I could do a few bodge jobs. A bit of Sellotape here and there. Bypass a few safety devices. Only if you want me to go down that route, could you put it in writing. If any of our customers are poisoned or electrocuted, I'd prefer it if you went to prison rather than me.'

'Now you're just being difficult.'

'Not at all. I'm just giving you the alternatives. And that only leaves one other.'

'And what might that be.'

'We tell our customers we can't repair their machines as we

can't afford spare parts. But keep giving us your money please. Now I'm no businessman, but I can't imagine many of them being too happy with that.'

'No, they won't. But I have to cut down on parts expenditure somehow.'

'I've given you my suggestions. You're the manager. You come up with something.'

This was one of the distractions he could do without on a day like this. And now he would have to deal with one of his customers who on past visits to this site hadn't been particularly offensive, but very irritating. He went to the reception and introduced himself with the words it seemed like he'd spoken a billion times.

'Good morning. I'm from Vendetta. I'm here to repair your vending machine.'

'Oh, wonderful. They'll be pleased to see you.'

'What seems to be the problem?'

'I was rather hoping you could tell us that.'

'I intend to, but what I meant was what are the symptoms? Is it any particular drink, or is it giving nothing at all?'

'It's giving out nothing. There's a message on the screen.'

'May I ask what the message says?'

'Waste bucket full.'

This would normally be an open goal for Barney, but he resisted the urge for a total barrage of sarcasm, mainly because she seemed like a nice young lady. Not that he was sexist. It was more that she was nice than that she was a lady. He'd had quite a few heated exchanges with some fearsome women during his career.

'That's telling you that the waste bucket inside the machine is full and has no room to take any more.'

'What's it full of?'

'Usually an enticing blend of cold tea, coffee, chocolate, and soup. Although there was one time when I found one full of... No, forget I said that.'

'How did the bucket become full?'

'Because people tip the drinks they don't want back into the machine, despite there being sink right next to it, and despite the notice on the front asking them not to.'

'So how do you fix it?'

'You empty the bucket.'

He liked getting jobs such as this. An easy task that should take just a few minutes. But he should have known better. It is never a good idea to assume a job is going to be easy. Over the years he had spent many hours doing getting stuck in places that he expected to be popping in and out of in ten minutes. The nice young lady took Barney to the coffee machine, which was in the middle of a busy office. He got his keys out and opened the machine door, and was greeted with the most horrendous smell imaginable. It was as if a hundred people had vomited at the same time. In fact, some people did exactly that as a handful of people sitting at their desks nearby ran to the toilet at high speed. Various noises of disapproval followed, as the revolting stink engulfed the entire office. Another lady, not so nice and not as young, with an expression on her face resembling a bulldog licking piss off a nettle came up to him and verbally laid into him.

'What the hell is going on? That smell is disgusting!'

Barney, who by now was getting a bit wound up replied, 'Oh really? I hadn't noticed.'

'You can't be serious. Can't you smell it?'

'Yes, of course I can smell it. How could I not smell it? There's an astronaut on the International Space Station complaining about it. There is a family of pigs on the farm up the road complaining about it.'

'Don't try to be funny with me. What are you going to do about it?'

'Strictly speaking, it's not my job. You are meant to empty the waste bucket yourselves. But on this occasion, I will do it as a gesture of good faith.'

The woman walked away without a word.

'You're welcome', muttered Barney.

The bucket was full to the brim. It obviously hadn't been emptied for a few weeks. The main component of the deadly cocktail was sour milk, which was the cause of the vile smell, and Barney struggled not to vomit himself. He wondered if some of the deaths attributed to vending machines in the radio feature were caused by catching a fatal disease due to the production of flesh-eating bacteria in the unemptied waste bucket. It wasn't going to be an easy task to carry out either. The bucket was heavy, and full to the very top. Much to his despair, there was a sign on the sink which told him it couldn't be used, as it was blocked.

He would somehow have to carry the bucket to the toilet, which was at the other end of the office to the machine. He would do well not to spill any on the carpet. Luckily the office was empty now. Most of the staff in the office couldn't bear the foul smell any longer and had escaped outside. He managed to get the bucket to the toilet without getting any on the carpet, but during the act of lifting the bucket up to the sink, he tipped a large amount all over his shirt and trousers. He quickly returned the empty bucket to the machine and locked it up. Back at reception a small crowd had gathered, and he had to endure a barrage of questions and insults. He took a great deal of pleasure in telling them that the smell would likely be hanging around for a few hours yet.

Outside, standing next to the car, he paused for some fresh air. But the vile smell was now attached to his clothes. He was feeling really down by this time. People were having a go at him for something which wasn't his fault. It was days like this that made him wish he didn't have to work. He had done this job for twenty-five years, ten at a company called Hot Cup where he was forced out after standing up to a racist customer, and fifteen at Vendetta. He'd had some good times, and often enjoyed what he was doing. But he was beginning to get fed up with it. He felt maybe it was time to look at doing something else. He had moments like this every now and then. Back in January he had been doing a job on a machine on the platform at Twyford railway station. It was bitterly cold and the repair took just over an hour. He wasn't feeling very well as he walked away from the machine. He was shivering, his hands were numb, and he was developing a nasty cough. And would anyone appreciate it? Or would someone come along later and beat the living daylights out of the machine because it hadn't given them their ten pence change? He decided then that he would definitely start looking for a different job. But his options were limited. Like most people who had always done a job which involved driving around from customer to customer, he would hate working in the same office all day. For a start he would struggle to stay awake, especially in the afternoon.

Despite the many moments when he'd decided enough was enough, he never went through with it. He always came back for more. It wasn't feasible to quit work. He owed a lot of money to some bad people. He had to somehow clear his debts before he could realistically think of taking a break from working. He couldn't in his wildest dreams have predicted what was to come two years later. He was to have an amazing stroke of good luck which would enable him to give up working forever

Prologue

Part 2

Four Years Ago

It was late summer, and the beginning of illuminations season at Blackpool. Barney, Alison, Mary, and Liam were having their first real get together since the wedding, and the birth of their son Jack. Daffy and Fiona from the darts team were also there, but the rest of the team couldn't make it. Tom was already on holiday in South Africa. He was spending his share of the twelve million pounds the darts team syndicate had won on the lottery, on travelling the world, and trying to find a girlfriend without much success. Roy had made some unconvincing excuse for not being there, but the truth was he hated Blackpool. That was the nature of Blackpool. Most people either loved it or loathed it. Barney had been there a few times and thought it was terrific. Mary and Alison had never been there, and Liam couldn't remember whether he had been or not. It was the first time for Daffy too, but Fiona had been there a few times when she was much younger and remembered it fondly. So for the majority of the gang, it was going to be a new experience.

It was going to be Alison's first night away from Jack, and she was already missing him, even though they had only been there for an hour. They had left him with Barney's mum Elizabeth in the bed and breakfast she ran in the Lake District, which wasn't all that far away if something went wrong, and they had to get back there. Alison was going to be phoning her far too frequently for everybody's liking, to the point where they were all fed up with it, and it was offending Elizabeth too. She knew how to look after difficult children. She was Barney's mother after all, and he was as much a pain as a kid as he is now as a grown up.

As often happened when the old gang met up, there was a bit of drinking involved, and soon after they had all checked in to the hotel, they gathered in a seafront pub. And as usual they stayed a lot longer than they first intended. Then Daffy complained he didn't come all this way to stay in one pub. He wanted to see what else was on offer. Mary pointed up to the sky and made a suggestion.

'I'd like to go up that tower.'

'Yes. Let's do that', was the general reply from most of them. Barney was the only one with objections.

'If you don't mind. I'll wait for you down on the ground.'

'Come on. Don't be such a miserable sod', said Mary.

'I'm not. But I will be miserable if I went up the tower. I'm not good with heights. I've only been up there once, and I hated it. My legs turned to jelly, I felt sick, and I came back down as quickly as I could.'

Alison asked him if she would like her to stay with him.

'No, no, I'll be fine. Don't worry about me. Just go and enjoy yourself. And I know how much you really want to go in there. And it's not just to go up the tower, is it?'

'No, it's not. You're not as daft as you look. But all the same, are you sure? I've heard sometimes you have to queue for hours. What are you going to do with yourself all that time?'

'Seriously?'

She instantly knew It was a daft question. Staring out to sea with a pint of beer in his hand was his idea of paradise.

Mary checked with Liam to confirm he was happy with the idea of going up the tower.

'Have you ever been up anything like this before?'

'I can't remember.'

It took them over two and a half hours altogether, mainly because Alison and Mary wanted to spend some time in the Tower Ballroom where the finals of Strictly Come Dancing were held. Mary in particular was a huge fan of the show. Daffy definitely wasn't. He looked around the room and asked, 'Is this the place where Anton Du Beke holds his balls and dances?'

'Very fucking funny', said Mary.

Mary desperately wanted to laugh, but fought hard to keep a straight face. She didn't want to give him the satisfaction. She had only met Daffy two or three times before, but his sense of humour wound her up, and she often gave him a hard time about it. In return, Daffy thought Mary was rather crude. But they secretly had a grudging admiration for each other.

They finally got up the tower, but had to queue for almost an hour. When they came back down, they found Barney still in the pub. He hadn't moved in all the time they had been away, and he was feeling quite merry.

By the time they all met up again, it was getting dark, and the illuminations were taking effect. They wandered along the golden mile and the debutants were impressed with the lights, the trams, and the general party atmosphere. The constant smell of fish and chips reminded them they hadn't eaten all day and were hungry. Daffy said, 'If only we could find a fish and chip shop somewhere around here.'

'You're quite the comedian today, aren't you?', said Mary.

'I try my best. Are your sides splitting?'

'Yes. Just look at me. I'm literally rolling around on the floor. Why do they call you Daffy, anyway?'

'They tell me it's because I'm amazing in bed. Some of my previous girlfriends named me after the legendary Roman emperor, Daffius the Orgasm Giver. Then they shortened it to just Daffy.'

'Do you have much success with women using lame chat up lines like that?'

'Nah, not really. I don't have a lot of success with women full stop come to think of it.'

'Well, what is the real reason they call you Daffy?'

'Because I once turned up at a darts match with a new haircut, and my hilarious mates in the team thought it made me look like Daffy Duck.'

'And did it?'

'No, I didn't think it did. But that wasn't going to stop them.'

'That's dithpicable.'

'Wow, I've never heard that before. Now who's the comedian?'

Barney listened to the conversation with interest. The way people reacted to haircuts was another aspect of human behaviour he never quite understood, even though he had played a large part in coming up with the Daffy nickname. He had a secret fear that one day an alien was going to beam down and ask him to explain why humans do some of the things they did. And if the alien asked him what the difference between men and women was, he would tell it that the biggest difference was the way they reacted to haircuts.

'You see, it's like this. If a female human gets her hair cut, the other female humans say things like, 'Ooooh, I like your hair', sometimes even when they don't like it. When a male human gets his hair cut, all the other male humans laugh at him and make up names of cartoon characters he may or may not look like, then call him that for the rest of his life.'

'How strange. Are there any other differences?'

'Yes. Some male humans think it's macho to fart. But most female humans only fart when they think nobody can hear.'

'Most interesting. It is a kind of mating ritual. The male tries to impress the female by breaking wind. Presumably as loud as possible?'

'No, mate. No. You've completely got the wrong end of the stick.'

'The wrong end of what stick?'

'The female won't be impressed. The male does it to impress the other males. And yes, as loud as possible, with an obnoxious smell thrown in for good measure.'

'Thank you, Earthling. You're a fascinating species. But I think

I'll just return to my own planet.'

The sarcasm from Daffy was justified. There were fish and chip shops everywhere. They headed for the one they liked the look of the most. Barney chipped in with some culinary advice.

'There's a local delicacy which I always have whenever I come here. I can highly recommend it.'

'What's it called?', asked Fiona.

'Chips and gravy.'

'Eat your heart out Jamie Oliver.'

They went into the fish and chip shop and ordered loads of stuff, some of them even trying the highly recommended chips and gravy, then continued the walk south along the promenade towards the pleasure beach. It took them quite a while, as they were all half drunk, and in Barney's case three quarters drunk, and wanted to stop and look at every distraction they encountered on the way, of which there were many. Barney couldn't understand how anybody couldn't like this place. Foreign visitors all go to London. Japanese tourists stand outside Buckingham Palace, or the Tower of London taking photographs. What the hell for? They'd have a far better time if they went to Blackpool. As they approached the Pleasure Beach, Mary looked in awe as the giant rollercoaster known as the Big One loomed ominously up ahead.

'Bloody hell! We're not going on that thing, are we? It's huge. Liam, have you been on that before? No wait. Don't bother answering that.'

Barney was the only one who said he wasn't going on it, for the same reasons he didn't go up the tower. They sampled some of the smaller rides first, which were scary enough themselves, then they had few more drinks to boost their courage levels and approached the entrance to the Big One. Mary surprisingly changed her mind at the last minute.

'Sorry. If you don't mind, I'm going to give it a miss. I'll stay down here and make sure Barney doesn't get into trouble.'

Alison wasn't having any of it.

'No way am I going to let you chicken out of this. Come on, let's go.'

'No. I can't.'

'Why not?'

'Because there's a sign at the entrance telling you not to go on if you're too small. Or if you're too young. Or if you've got a heart condition. Or if you're pregnant.'

'But none of us are too small, or too young, or have a heart condition, well apart from me obviously, and I'm willing to take the risk. And as far as we know, none of us are pregnant, are we?'

Mary looked at Alison in silence with a blank expression, and then a huge smile came across her face. Alison paused and looked back at her, and then at last it suddenly dawned on her.

'Oh my god! You are!'

'Yes, I am. Why do you think I was drinking cokes in the pub?'

Alison hugged her.

I'm going to say to you exactly what you said to me when I told you I was pregnant.'

'What was that?'

'Congratu fucking lations!'

The rest of the crowd passed on their congratulations too, all repeating that same phrase, then went on the rollercoaster while Barney and Mary stayed with their feet firmly on the ground and chatted.

'Are you really pregnant, or did you just need an excuse to not go on that thing?'

'I really am. But I was glad to get out of it. I could have done it. But I got a bigger thrill going to the ballroom where Strictly Come Dancing took place.'

'Alison would have been thrilled with that too.'

'She was. Do you watch strictly?'

'I've been forced to see bits of it while Alison was watching it.'

'It's really great. You should try watching it.'

'I would rather cover my balls with essence of hazelnut and shove a family of hungry squirrels down my trousers.'

'Whatever turns you on. Why don't you like it? Although I must admit, I can't see you as a dancer.'

'I've had my moments. I've jumped around a few times at gigs and discos. But I think dancing is about how you feel when you're doing it, not what it looks like to other people. That's one of the reasons I don't like Strictly.'

'It's just a bit of fun.'

'It's more than that to some. What kind of country do we live in where a front page of a newspaper tells you that the biggest news of the day is someone who doesn't deserve it has been voted off a dance show, then you turn to page two and read ten thousand people have died in an earthquake?'

They changed the subject. She asked him how life was.

'Not too bad. Jack can be difficult at times, and one of the cats hates me. But at least I don't have to deal with vending machine users any longer.'

He deliberately avoided talking about Alison. He knew anything he said would get back to her. Mary was not the best person to share any secrets with.

'I bet you miss work really.'

'No, I don't. Not in the slightest.'

'Don't you get bored? You're very young to retire.'

'No, not at all.'

'Come off it. You don't fool me. I bet you miss the enjoyment of all those arguments with customers, and your bosses.'

'You couldn't be more wrong. People have this misconception about me. I would have been much happier at work if everyone was nice to each other, and I had just gone home contented with my day's work. Instead, I used to go home feeling guilty and wondering if I'd gone too far.'

'Then why are you so confrontational?'

'I have a strong sense of what is right and wrong. I hate workplace bullies. I refuse to stay quiet while other people make my life unnecessarily difficult through their power crazed actions, selfish behaviour, or sheer stupidity. Not just at work. I mean life in general.'

'Liam says he's often seen you get worked up about things which are not worth caring about.'

'Not to him maybe. There is a song called The Only One by one of my favourite bands, Stiff Little Fingers. The lyrics could have been written especially for me. It tells you that if something makes you angry, even if you are the only person in the world that gets angry about it, it is still a worthwhile cause and you're not wrong for acting on it. What you feel is real. It also tells you at the end of the song you are not the only one. There will always be someone somewhere who feels the same. If I was feeling down after I'd had arguments at work, I used to play the song when I was driving home. It gave me a great deal of comfort.'

'Wow! I've never heard you talk like this before. It's nice to see you have a sensitive side.'

'Thanks Mary.'

'I've always thought you were just an argumentative bastard.'

'Thanks Mary.'

'I still think you'll regret giving up work so soon.'

'Not a chance. I have no intentions of ever working again.'

1

Present Day

Alison and Barney were in the ski resort of Les Arcs in France. It was four years after the Blackpool outing, when they had for the first time gone away for the night and left Jack with Barney's mum. They had done the same a few times since then, but this holiday was a much bigger step. They were leaving him for the whole week. Alison was worried. Not because she thought anything would happen to him, but because she was worried that she would miss him too much.

Although Alison thought her son was the greatest thing in the world, Jack wasn't the easiest child to be a parent to. He clearly had some learning difficulties, but they had no official diagnosis yet. It was a long, slow process. They had managed a few holidays. Perhaps 'managed' isn't the right word in their case as most people would say it's easy to go on holiday when you don't have work commitments to get in the way, and you've got a couple of million quid in the bank. They went to places such as Disneyland, and to seaside resorts in countries such as Spain and Greece, but they couldn't have a relaxing time with Jack around. They also resisted the temptation to invite any friends along, too. This was just going to be the two of them. But Alison was still going to miss him terribly.

It hadn't been a smooth handover of Jack. Barney had a row with his mum, which wasn't a rare event by any means. Alison was piggy in the middle and tried to act as peacemaker, but didn't do a very good job. It all started when Elizabeth said she was looking forward to taking him to church on Sunday. Barney wasn't best pleased at the idea.

'Why are you taking him to church?'

'I go to church every Sunday. I can't leave him at home on his own.'

'Would it harm you to give it a miss just once? Is God going to be that bothered? He's got a lot more things he should be sorting out without stressing that you've missed church for the first time in about six decades.'

'I'm not going to give it a miss. If you don't like it, find someone else to look after him.'

'Just keep him away from your religious crackpot mates. I don't want them trying fill his head with nonsense.'

'My friends are not crackpots. They are friendly and kind. Jack will benefit from meeting them, instead of constantly having to listen to someone argumentative and rude like you.'

At this point Alison could see things were getting heated, and thought it was time to intervene and try to calm things down.

'I don't see any problem with your mum taking Jack to church. After all, he's only four years old. He's not going to understand any of that mumbo jumbo.'

Now it was Alison's turn to feel Elizabeth's wrath.

'It is not mumbo jumbo, and I'd appreciate it if you didn't say things like that.'

'I'm sorry Elizabeth. I didn't mean it to come out like that. I was just trying to say it's fine by me if you take Jack to church.'

Barney found Alison's foot in mouth moment hilarious and

started to laugh, much to the annoyance of the other two, and they both had a go at him. He knew it was time to give in.

'Okay. Take him to church. But when I come to collect him next week, he'd better not have turned into some kind of born again wackadoodle.'

Despite the argument, there was no question of them not leaving Jack with Elizabeth. She loved having her grandson stay, and they didn't have anyone else to do it.

Barney didn't share the same worries about leaving Jack. His concerns were more to do with the type of holiday they had embarked upon. It was Alison's suggestion that they went skiing. Barney's initial response wasn't one of complete enthusiasm.

There were two things Barney had vowed never to do. They were horse riding and skiing. Alison had tried to persuade him to go horse riding with her before. But he politely declined.

'I don't even want to stand anywhere near an enormous beast with huge sharp teeth and with great big lumps of metal nailed to its feet, let alone climb on the back of one.'

'But they're such magnificent creatures.'

'What's magnificent about them? They're just the same as cows. They eat grass and fart a lot but at least cows give me milk for my Coco Pops, not to mention the occasional quarter pounder with cheese.'

'They are nothing like cows. Do you remember that time you went to Windsor races with Mary? Imagine how exciting it would have been if it was cows racing.'

'I might have had a better chance at picking a winner. But I get your point. Then again, I don't mind watching horses having a race. I've no problem if they are being driven by four foot eleven, seven stone Irishmen, but I don't want to do it myself.'

The suggestion of a skiing holiday had brought a similar reluctance from Barney.

'You must be bloody joking! There's not a snowflake's chance in hell of me going skiing. If you think I'm going to hurtle down the side of a mountain at breakneck speed with a plank of wood tied to each foot, you'd better think again. And I don't much relish sitting in a chair up in the sky dangling from a flimsy piece of wire either.'

But Alison's powers of persuasion were strong. She knew she was on to a loser with the horse riding. But she got him to agree to the skiing in the end. It was an odd reversal of their past lifestyles. Barney had always played competitive sports ever since he was a schoolboy. That was mainly football, cricket, swimming, a bit of athletics, and of course darts. But skiing was something else. His fear of heights might have been a key factor in his reluctance.

Alison on the other hand had never been sporty. At school she was always the last one to get picked for the team. But she was very fit. After her divorce from her controlling husband, she started going to the gym for a workout most days and had kicked her forty a day cigarette habit. She had always liked the idea of going skiing, but could never really afford it. And now she could. She was very clever. She played on Barney's weaknesses. She had convinced him that he would enjoy the après-ski, and also how much he would love the scenery.

So here they were. They started off the week skiing together, as they were at this point on the same level. They hired a private instructor, a tall, handsome Frenchman called Jacques with an accent that made Alison go weak at the knees (not a good condition for skiing). Barney had to remind her to stop skiing with her tongue hanging out several times.

'You should hear yourself. Ooooh, I love your accent. I've got a boy called Jack too. He has lovely blond curly hair, just like yours.'

'I didn't have you down as the jealous type.'

'I'm not jealous. I'm just concerned that if you drool much more, you'll ruin the snow for everybody.'

Their opposing levels of enthusiasm were reflected in the progress of their skiing skills. Neither of them had been on a skiing holiday before, but Alison at least had a few practice sessions on an artificial ski slope back at home, so she had a head start. By the third day, she was doing red runs, and was determined to do a black run by the end of the week. Barney by contrast was still struggling to master the blues and greens, and had taken a few tumbles. Jacques told them there was no point in teaching them both at the same time. They needed different kinds of tuition. He suggested getting one of his mates to take over the tutoring of Barney. Barney was convinced that Jacques just wanted to get Alison on her own, but in terms of learning to ski, he knew it would be for the best.

The next morning, Alison disappeared into the distance with her dream instructor, while Barney was introduced to his new tutor. He had been hoping for a hot French girl, and give Alison a taste of her own medicine, but it didn't happen. Only the French part was right.

'Allo. They call me Mad Pierre.'

'Why do they call you that?'

'Because Pierre is my name. And I'm mad.'

'I suppose I should have worked that one out.'

'Okay my friend. What would you like to do first?'

'I'd like to go for coffee and croissants.'

'Zis is a most unusual request. Don't you want to learn to ski?'

'To be honest, I'm not too sure whether I do or not. Especially by someone who tells me he is mad. But I definitely want coffee and croissants. And I'm paying for this. So that's what we are going to do.'

'You are ze boss.'

They went for the coffee and croissants and got to know each other. Then they eventually went skiing. Mad Pierre turned out to be a good teacher. They spent two hours doing the easiest runs, but the experience boosted Barney's confidence and he began to enjoy it. Mad Pierre was encouraging him.

'You are getting better. Soon you will be winning a gold medal for Great Britain at the winter Olympics.'

'Do you think so?'

'Yes. In the Green Run, Slightly Downhill, Eddie the Eagle Embarrassing Englishman category. I think you are ready to try something a little more difficult.'

'Non. I'm ready to try something a leetle less difficult, Monsieur Mad. I'd like to try 'ow you say entrecote frites and un beer or deux.'

'Your stereotypical portrayal of the French is 'ow you say insulting, your attempts to speak French are 'ow you say shit, and your attempts to ski are 'ow you say even shitter, Mister Smartarse.'

'In many ways you remind me of me Mad Pierre. So, what do you think of the suggestion?'

'Absolutely old chap. Spiffing. I say, a steak and chips, and a beer or two would be jolly super. Rather smashing in fact. How do you do?'

'Wouldn't you rather go for some snails? Or maybe a frog sandwich?'

'No. An English style overcooked steak will be just fine. I know a place that will burn it black for you, or make it taste like you are eating rubber.'

Despite all his sarcasm, Mad Pierre didn't mind the suggestion at all. The French liked to have long lunches. The pistes were very quiet for a couple of hours in the early part of the afternoon. Alison, like many of British visitors and other nationalities, took the opportunity to do a lot of skiing during this period. Barney opted for the French tradition of having long lunches. Sitting with half a litre of beer in his hand staring at the snow-covered mountains was another one of his ideas of paradise. Alison had been clever in selling the skiing holiday idea this way. She knew that he loved being by mountains, valleys, lakes, rivers, and oceans. He'd never seen anything quite like this before other than on postcards and television. It looked incredible. Being somewhere like this was like resetting his brain. Installing some calm to an otherwise aggressive mind.

They had their steak and chips and a few beers. More than a few. Even a hardened drinker like Barney was struggling to keep up with Mad Pierre. They were both getting seriously drunk. Then Mad Pierre told him it was time for some action.

'Right. Let's go and do some black runs.'

'I don't think so. You might be mad, but I'm not. Besides, it's getting dark. The chair lifts appear to be closing.'

'Ah. We've been here longer than I thought. Maybe we can come back and tackle some black runs in the morning? Let's have another beer.'

'I'll go along with that. The beer I mean, not the black runs.'

'You can do a black run. All you've got to do is zigzag your way down. Just watch out for the crocodiles.'

'I will. Do you… wait a minute. Crocodiles?'

'Oui. Do you know why skiers zigzag?'

'No.'

'It's to escape from crocodiles. They are fast in a straight line but can't turn quickly. If one chases you, you have to zigzag.'

'I'll remember that. Any other pearls of wisdom?'

'Yes. The muscles which close a crocodile's jaws are very powerful. But the muscles that open its jaws are weak and feeble. If one of them catches you, just put your finger on its nose. Then it can't eat you.'

'Do you get many crocodiles up here in the Alps?'

'We used to. But now they are extinct. They couldn't catch the zigzagging skiers. Also, people started carrying elastic bands to put over their noses. They all starved to death.'

Barney started laughing and then fell of his chair. Mad Pierre helped him up and suggested they call it a day.

Over the next two days, Alison was becoming very proficient, and while Barney had improved under Mad Pierre somewhat, although he was finding out that his nickname was justified. But he had reached his level and was destined to be an eternal intermediate. Mad Pierre's prediction of Olympic gold was somewhat over-optimistic, even in the made-up category.

On the last night, the holiday company were advertising a 'Hot Rock and Torchlit Descent.' They both liked the look of it and bought tickets, without checking exactly what was involved. All they knew was It took place in a restaurant halfway up a mountain. The idea was to stay up the mountain after their day skiing and go straight to the restaurant. The meal consisted mainly of large slabs of meat thrown onto a huge hot stone. That was right up Barney's street. So was the unlimited supply of wine that was included in the price.

There were ten others in the group, mainly English holidaymakers. Barney found them surprisingly sociable. He was expecting a bunch of chinless Ruperts, or hooray Henrys and Henriettas. But they weren't. They were mainly just the same as him and Alison. Not quite the same though. They were probably fairly affluent to be able to afford to go skiing, but Barney and Alison were the only millionaires. Not that they mentioned it. It all resulted in a very enjoyable evening.

They both took advantage of the unlimited wine and were getting drunk, even before they played the nose game. The nose game was a ridiculous, and simple idea dreamed up by one of holiday reps, but it worked well and was really funny. The rules, or just one rule, was when one of the group touched their nose with their finger, ideally during a conversation while nobody was expecting it, everyone else had to touch their nose. The last person to do it had to drink two fingers of wine. It got chaotic at times and a lot of wine was consumed.

At the end of the evening, the rep explained the details of the torchlit descent. She told them if anyone was too tired or drunk to ski down, they could go down on the sledge. Alison asked Barney if he would like to do that. Barney mistakenly assumed that it would be the sort of sledge he got for Christmas when he was eight years old.

'There's no way I can drive a sledge in my state. Besides, I'm an ace skier now. Just watch me go.'

'It's not that sort of sledge, dumb arse. It's a big vehicle with an engine and seats in the back. Someone else will be driving it. You can sit there and enjoy the ride.'

'No way. I'm going to ski down.'

The rep then explained that there were five torches between the twelve skiers. She asked for volunteers to be torch carriers. Barney steamed in.

'I'll have some of that. I'll be a torch carrier.'

But his enthusiasm diminished when he saw that the torches weren't little battery-operated hand-held devices. They consisted of a large metal pot of fire dangling from a chain with a wooden handle. Alison checked that Barney felt up to the task. But he was full of wine fuelled courage, and he didn't want to back out and look foolish.

In terms of looking foolish, it would have been a better option to back out. The pot of fire was heavier than it looked. He only got as far as the first bend, then he lost balance and tumbled over. Then the pot of fire set his cheap ski pants alight. He was so full of alcohol, it was a wonder that he didn't completely ignite. He lay there helpless, but found the whole situation hilarious. He was singing 'I'm on Fire' by Kasabian, while the others sprang into action and beat the flames out and threw snow on him. He didn't feel any pain as it was happening, but he would have a few sore spots in the morning. The speed of his rescuers saved him from any real harm but couldn't save his trousers. They were now full of holes, and large areas of his legs were exposed. The rep insisted he go down in the sledge, and he wasn't about to argue this time.

It was an enjoyable ride back down to the resort, and he changed the song he was singing to Jingle Bells. He watched Alison ski all the way down, half hoping she would fall, but by now she was too good, even while drunk.

The next day was their last one. They had to leave for the airport at noon, so Alison had one final ski. She achieved her target of doing a black run with the help of Jacques. Barney had a lie in and told Mad Pierre he might as well do the same. He didn't have any trousers to go skiing in.

2

Barney was at Lords cricket ground in London. It was the third day of a test match between England and South Africa. He was treating his dad, Cecil Barnard senior, to a day watching cricket. The last time they both went to a test match together was five years ago, when Barney bought tickets for his dad's seventieth birthday. That time the venue was the Oval, and Barney had got himself in trouble with his boss, because he had phoned in to say he was sick, but was spotted on television in the crowd.

Today he would not have the same problem. He was now retired. Thanks to a lottery win by his darts team syndicate, he was now a millionaire. His day out wouldn't be constantly interrupted by phone calls from work mates asking stupid questions this time. Or so he thought. In fact, he would later receive a call from his old service desk coordinator, Mary. And the question she was going to ask was way beyond stupid.

Barney had resisted the urge to hire a hospitality box, even though he could easily afford it. He was against it in principle. He imagined they were hired by businesses and were probably full of knobheads who had no interest in the cricket, and were purely there to drink as much free booze as they could. So, as usual they were sitting out in the open air among the average punters, although the prices of even the cheapest tickets, not to mention the prices of the drinks were so outrageous, he wondered how the non-millionaires he was mingling with could afford to come.

It wasn't an ideal day for watching cricket. It was cloudy, and a strong breeze was blowing across the ground. The game had progressed slowly and was not going well for England. They had been bowled out on the first day for 263, which South Africa matched on day two for the loss of 4 wickets. South Africa would be looking to bat for the majority of today, which wasn't what Barney had come to see. By the lunch break no further wickets had fallen, but the run rate was painfully slow. At least it gave the two of them a chance to have a chat and catch up with any news.

Cecil enquired, 'So where's the lovely Alison today? Would she not have liked to come along?'

Barney faked a puzzled look. 'I'm sorry, I don't know who you mean.'

'Very funny. Alison is lovely. You're lucky to be married to her. I hope you don't do anything stupid to ruin things.'

'Oh, so you're an expert in marriage now. How did yours work out?'

'That's a bit below the belt. Even by your standards.'

'I know. Sorry.'

'Your mum and I were happy together. But eventually realised we were even happier not together. Times were tough. We didn't have much money, which is thankfully a problem you won't have. It's not easy raising kids. Especially when your only son is such a cantankerous sod.'

'Oh, that's charming!', replied Barney with indignation. But then they both laughed.

'How is your mum by the way? I haven't seen her since your wedding, and we just briefly said a polite hello.'

'She's fine. Still running the bed and breakfast. Still going to church every Sunday. She is trying to claim it was her prayers that won us the lottery. I see a lot more of her these days. Our house is only thirty miles from hers. It's handy because Jack likes having a sleepover now and then, which is useful if we both have to go out somewhere.'

'How's the darts going? Do you still play for a team?'

'Not very often these days. When I first moved to the Lake District, I would travel down to London and play for the team three or four times a season. Now I try to fit in at least one game a year.'

'Are there no teams near where you live.'

'I tried playing for a pub which was ten miles from our village. That was the nearest I could find. But it just wasn't the same. Our team are all great friends. It was difficult trying to get to know a team of strangers. And there was no way of getting home from the pub on public transport, so I had to take the car. I couldn't even have a drink.'

'You can play darts without having a drink.'

'On what planet? Why do you think darts matches take place in pubs? No, I've given up the idea of finding a new team. My old team still do a trip somewhere every year, and that usually includes a prearranged friendly darts game with some locals, wherever that may be.'

'Back to my original question, did Alison not want to come today? It would have been lovely to see her.'

'No. She doesn't like cricket. I took her to Old Trafford last year and she was bored stiff. We had to leave halfway through the game. And that was a one day international, with sixes and fours flying everywhere, and stumps getting flattened every ten minutes. Just imagine how bored she would be watching this one. Besides, we have a cantankerous sod of our own who needs looking after. So we couldn't have both been here.'

'How is young Jack?'

'He's still a bit of a handful. But he can't do anything wrong as far as Alison is concerned. The pair of them, and those two bloody cats drive me round the bend. We'll all come down for a visit soon. Not the cats obviously. But the rest of us. We'll pencil in a date before I go back tomorrow.'

Alison used to work at Vendetta. Soon after the lottery win, they quit their jobs and got married. They both sold their houses, which made them even wealthier, then they bought a relatively modest house, in a beautiful location in the Lake District, an area he used to visit frequently to see his mum who ran a bed and breakfast, and to get a free holiday. They had a son, Jack, which came as a huge surprise and relief to Alison who had given up any hope of having children.

The game became a bit more interesting after the lunch break. England took three quick wickets, and the pair did less chatting, and more watching. Just after the tea break there was a hold up in play because one of the England players fielding close to the batsman, got hit right in the crown jewels off a full-blooded pull shot and fell to the ground like a sack of potatoes. As he rolled around in agony clutching his groin, the rest of the players were laughing like naughty schoolboys.

Barney was often perplexed by the behaviour of some members of the human race. He had seen this happen on the cricket field many times before, but just couldn't understand it. If the player had been struck on the elbow, or ankle, or chest, the other players would run up to him, ask if he was ok, and call for the physio. But get one in the balls, where it hurts the most, and your teammates turn into giggling imbeciles and find the agony of the victim hilarious. This could well be another thing he would have to explain to the alien.

The game eventually got going again. Then about half an hour before the close of play, Barney's phone rang. His ringtone was Action by Def Leppard. He was by no means a fan of Def Leppard, but liked the intro of that particular song. The problem was it was very loud, and not at all welcome at a cricket match. He had forgotten to turn the ringtone off, which is the sort of thing that would have infuriated him if someone else had done it. A few of the other spectators made their feeling known with loud tuts and mumbled comments. The name 'Sweary' flashed up on the screen. Sweary was the nickname the engineers had given Mary, obviously because she liked to swear a lot, particularly at them. But she was alright when you got to know her. She could be quite funny at times, and that was the sort of thing that would help Barney get through each day. He was puzzled though. She didn't normally call him. They have met up for drinks a few times, but that would usually be arranged by Alison, and by E mail. He apprehensively answered the call. She didn't sound like the usual abrasive character he knew. In fact, she sounded flustered, and even a bit desperate. But he wasn't expecting her to say what she said next.

'Barney, I need you to come back to work!'

3

At first glance, Kenneth appeared to be a weedy little man. The terms 'nerd', or 'geek' would be the stereotypical way of describing him, although these words suggest some kind of super intelligence, but Kenneth wasn't all that bright either. It would be more accurate to say he was quite clever, but lacked common sense. What he did have was a nasty streak. He'd had that for quite a while, but as he was soon to demonstrate, he actually was a very evil man, capable of much worse actions than anyone could imagine.

He didn't like going out much and spent most of his time sitting staring at a computer screen with his curtains closed. He didn't have any friends or family, or at least any family that wanted anything to do with him. He had been married twice before, but neither of the marriages had lasted. His first time was to a woman he had met through a dating site and had only lasted a few months. The second wife was someone he had met at a bus stop while waiting for a bus. It lasted longer than the first one, but ultimately also ended in failure. Today, he was indulging in one of his favourite pastimes, trawling social media, looking for targets for his spite and malice. He would be proud to be referred to as a troll. He got a kick from watching people suffer.

He spotted a post on Facebook reporting how an eighty-year-old woman had her bike stolen while she popped into the supermarket. This was followed a string of typical responses from the keyboard warriors.

'What a disgusting thing to do.'

'I no. they should of striped him naked and tide him up in the high street'

'Yes. Then gave him a hundred lashes with a wip.'

'and then they should of left him to starve to death LOL'

'How do you know it was a man? That's typical of a woman to assume he's a man. How do you know it wasn't a woman who stole his bike?'

'You say I assume he was a man, yet you assume I'm a woman,'

'I assumed you were a woman because your name is Laura.'

'I know it's a man because they caught him on CCTV. He's been arrested. LMFAO'

'what is england coming to it's a digrase'

'I blame the parents you shouldnt be allowed to have kids if this is how you bring them up theres no respect these days my parents would of spanked me with a shoe if I did this and sent me to bed without any food im so disgusted'

'what cn anyone and be away to that'

'What the hell are you talking about?'

'Oh, here come the grammer police.'

'It's nothing to do with grammer, or even grammar. I just don't know what the hell you're talking about.'

'its time they brought back the death penalty. Hanging is too good for scum like this.'

'Hanging IS the death penalty. Make your mind up. Should they bring it back, or is it too good for him? What method of execution do you advocate?'

'this is disgusting how would you feel if it was your own grandmother they should lock him up and throw away the key I carnt believe someone could do this'

'I no.it makes my blood boil that people like this are walking round freely.'

'I agree. What a waste of oxygen.'

'Karma will get him'

'No it won't. That isn't even a real thing. You are a prat if you think that's a real thing. It's not even a real thing.'

'Yes it is. and it will get him.'

At this point Kenneth couldn't resist joining in. It was time to have a bit of fun and wind some of these idiots up.

'It serves the silly cow right. If you are stupid enough to leave your bike unlocked, you deserve everything you get.'

This prompted a number of abusive responses, which Kenneth enjoyed immensely. He couldn't explain why, but he got a real kick out of this. But the kick didn't last long and he soon got bored and turned his attention elsewhere.

He spent twenty minutes on a sex chat website but wasn't really in the mood to enjoy it so he left it and returned to Facebook where he read a news article about Katie Price. As usual there was a vicious tirade of abuse aimed at her.

'This woman is just a desperate publicity seeker.'

'I know. Why is she even on the news.'

'WTF Cos she thinks we all want to read about her.'

'But you are reading about her LMAO.'

'Only because I wanted to see what shed been saying but I'm not interested in what shes been saying.'

'The woman is just an attention seeker LOL.'

'I think she might have had plastic surgery.'

'No shit Sherlock.'

Kenneth intervened.

'Leave her alone. You're all just jealous because she's beautiful and rich and famous, and you're just a bunch of talentless losers.'

But nobody took the bait, so he left Facebook and went on a job recruitment website instead. He was temporarily out of work and was on the lookout for new employment. At first there wasn't much to interest him. Then something caught his eye. The vending machine company Vendetta was looking for engineers to repair machines, and operators to fill and clean them. He was familiar with Vendetta, and even more familiar with some of their employees. This prompted him to enter a search for the name Cecil Barnard, but he found nothing he didn't already know. He wondered if he still worked at Vendetta. He filled out an application for the engineer job. But it wasn't work that he had in mind. It was revenge. He had a score to settle.

4

The phone call from Mary had taken him by surprise. Such was his surprise, he reacted by telling her he was unable to speak to her at that moment and promised to call her back in the evening. She had said, 'Barney, I need you to come back to work.' He wondered why she would say such a thing. It didn't make any sense. She sounded stressed when she said it.

It was close of play at Lords, and England had finished the day strongly. They had bowled out South Africa who had a lead of nearly two hundred, but had batted well in reply and hadn't lost any wickets when bad light called a halt to the day twenty minutes early. They took the train back to Barney's dad's house. Cecil senior was seventy-five years old, and the long day had worn him out, so he went straight to bed. It was still a bit early for Barney, so he decided to pop out to the pub for an hour or two. While he was there, he would call Mary and find out exactly what it was she wanted. Mary and Barney had a bit of a love/hate relationship when they worked together. It took some time for Barney to realise that the more Mary was rude to you, the more she liked you. He felt at times she must really like him a lot.

It took Mary less than two seconds to answer his call. It was as if she was waiting for him. She didn't sound as stressed as she had earlier, but she still wasn't quite herself. They weren't usually polite to each other on the phone, but he sensed this wasn't the time to be taking the piss out of each other. The opening to the call was the most civilised conversation they had ever had.

'Hi Mary. Sorry I couldn't talk earlier. I was at Lords, watching the cricket with my dad.'

'That's ok. Sorry to have disturbed you.'

'Is everything ok?'

'No. I'm having a lot of problems at work.'

'Ok, I'm not sure how I can help, but tell me all about it.'

'The two big chiefs left the company unexpectedly last month, leaving Richard Bowles in charge. Then last week, Richard was taken seriously ill. He's going to be off for a few weeks. This means that as the next most senior person in the depot, I am now temporarily in charge. But it's been a disaster. We haven't got enough staff, and some of them are taking no notice of anything I say. We have some new trainees, but most of them are useless, and we have nobody to train them properly. The company is falling apart. That's why I said earlier that I needed you to come back to work. It would just be for a few weeks until I get through this crisis. You could help in whatever form you choose.'

'How much would I get paid?'

'Oh, I didn't think of that. I assumed being a millionaire you wouldn't need the money.'

'I don't. And I don't need the hassle either. I'm happily retired. And I intend to stay that way, as tempting as your offer may be. I've been doing this job for many years. I've had electric shocks, scalded myself, cut my hands more times than I could count, got covered in all kinds of foul smelling liquids, been moaned at, laughed at, shouted at, sworn at, barged into, and had umpteen complaints about my attitude, and been warned about my conduct. I've had speeding tickets, parking tickets, and have been sent home and lost half a days pay for having a dirty car. I have even been warned for not ironing my trousers. That's hardly my fault. I don't even own an iron. I've had some good times along the way too. I've worked for some good bosses and there have been plenty of decent customers who I've enjoyed dealing with. And best of all I've made some fantastic friends. But I've had enough. Like I told you in Blackpool a few years back, I have no intentions of ever working again.'

'Ok. I knew it was a long shot. Would you a least think about it?'

'Alright. I'll think about it', he said, but obviously didn't mean it.

'Thanks. See you later.'

Then she ended the call. Barney decided to have one more pint before going back for a sleep. But fifteen minutes after ending the call with Mary, the phone played another burst of Action by Def Leppard. It was Alison. The conversation that followed wasn't really a conversation. It was one person talking loudly at the other one who couldn't get a word in.

'What the hell's wrong with you, you heartless bastard? I've just had Mary on the phone. She's crying her eyes out. She's our friend. It doesn't matter how much money we have. Would it kill you to show a bit of compassion and help a friend in need? I have already told her I'll go back myself for a few weeks, as soon as I sort out some childcare. If you had an ounce of decency, you'd do the same.'

Then Alison abruptly ended the call.

'Hello dear, how are you? Have you had a nice day?', mumbled

Barney to himself.

He sat for ten minutes contemplating his next action. But deep down he knew what he had to do. He called Mary back.

'Ok, I've decided I'll return to work. But not for too long. Just two weeks, or maybe three at the most.'

'Oh, that's brilliant. Thanks. What persuaded you to change your mind?'

'Don't give me that load of old bollocks. You know fine well what, or to be more accurate, who persuaded me to change my mind. And I still haven't changed it. I'd still rather not work. That must have been some performance you put on. Boo hoo, I'm so desperate. Please help. Wah wah.'

'It wasn't like that.'

'Have you been nominated for an Oscar yet?'

'You can be so cruel sometimes.'

'Hello! This is me you're talking to. How long have we known each other?'

'Fair point. Welcome back, dickhead.'

5

Barney was back home in the Lake District. It was Saturday, and although all days were pretty much the same these days, this one felt like a more traditional Saturday where he had to get as much enjoyment in as he possibly could because he was back at work on Monday. It wasn't a feeling he thought he would ever have to endure again. It wasn't a feeling he was enjoying. He contemplated a stroll around the lake, followed by a visit to his local for a couple of pints and watch a bit of sport. But Alison had other ideas.

'I need to drive into town and do some shopping. I have to buy some things for Jack, and a few other bits and pieces if I'm returning to work.'

'You know I would have helped Mary out anyway, didn't you? There was no need for you to give me all that hassle.'

'I know. You eventually get around to doing the right thing. But sometimes you just need a little shove in the right direction.'

'That must have been some performance from Mary.'

'Don't be too harsh on her. It wasn't all an act. Some of her tears were genuine. She has been left with a huge responsibility she didn't ask for, and is desperate to succeed. Besides, you're always banging on about how important friends are. A friend in need and all that.'

'Yeah, okay. I've agreed to do it. But I don't have to be happy about it.'

She gave him a goodbye kiss.

'Can I trust you to amuse Jack for a few hours? Oh, and don't forget to feed George and Mildred.'

'Why should I feed them? One of them tolerates me, and the other one hates me.'

'She'll hate you even more if you don't feed her.'

Alison left for the shops. But just because he had been robbed of his trip to the pub, he wasn't going to let it spoil his afternoon. It was the time of year when the football and cricket seasons overlapped, so there was plenty sport to watch, and as always, there was a fridge full of lager. He cracked open the first one, then decided to feed the cats now, otherwise he would forget, and then he would be in big trouble.

Alison had named the cats George and Mildred after a sitcom from the nineteen seventies, an era when it was considered to be hilarious if any of the characters were black or gay, and sexual stereotypes were everywhere. She had inadvertently stumbled across it on a channel such as Dave, or ITV4. It was a harmless, if not particularly hilarious comedy, a spin off from Man About the House, (another harmless but not particularly hilarious sitcom but arguably slightly funnier than it's spin off) about the Ropers, who were a henpecked useless husband and a dominant wife. It was understandable why she took a liking to it, given the nature of her first marriage. Life hadn't always been the way it was now for her. She had been married before, but it hadn't been a happy time. Her husband was a bully and controlled everything she did and everywhere she went. For years she lived an oppressed life, until the death of her parents had sparked an angry reaction in her and she found the strength to divorce her husband. Barney understood that much of her bossiness now was brought about because she was determined not to let history repeat itself. There was never any chance of that happening, but Barney gave her a lot of leeway, and he didn't mind the situation. He just wanted an easy life. The main reason he asked her to marry him in the first place (other than the fact that he was completely off his face on free booze at the Vendetta Christmas party and was rolling around the floor in a semi trance after receiving the news he had won millions of pounds) was how much he admired the way she had fought back from the oppression she had suffered and regained her confidence to rebuild her life. Therefore, he could hardly complain when she expressed her opinions forcefully. But sometimes he had a feeling Alison was turning into Mildred, and he had to play the role of George Roper.

He put the cat food in the bowls. George crept up and started to eat. Mildred stayed under the table and hissed at Barney as he walked past. She would go to the food once he had gone out of the room. To celebrate the completion of the first task, he downed another can of lager. Then turned his attention to Jack, his four-year-old son. Jack wasn't quite as hostile to Barney as Mildred was, but he was a real mummy's boy.

'Where's mummy gone?' asked Jack.

'She's just gone into town to go shopping.'

'When is she coming back?'

'She'll be back later. Is there anything you want?'

'Crisps.'

'Ok. I'll get you some crisps.'

He wolfed them down.

'Can I have some more please?'

Barney knew he was too soft, but he just wanted to get back to his can of beer and his television.

'Ok, I'll let you have some more, but I don't want any of your usual snitching. You mustn't tell mummy you had more than one packet.'

'I'll not tell mummy.'

Barney defiantly gave him two more packets of crisps. He was working on the principal that he was about to drink far more than the recommended safe units of alcohol, so it would have been hypocritical of him to deprive Jack of his excessive crisp feast just because some boring nutritional experts bang on about how bad they are for you.

'Is there anything you want to do?'

'Can I do some painting?'

'Yes. I don't mind you doing painting. But you have to do it on the kitchen table and cover it with old newspaper. You mustn't make a mess. If mummy comes home and the place is a mess, she will be very cross. And you know who she would be most cross with, don't you?'

'Yes. You daddy.'

'I was going to say you, but who am I kidding?'

He set up the painting set on the kitchen table and retired to the sofa with yet another can of beer. He could see the top of Jack's head from where he was lying. Hopefully he could keep an eye on him, while watching the telly at the same time. This happy arrangement lasted for most of the afternoon. Barney drifted off to sleep at one stage and woke up as the final scores were coming through. Once he had heard the results that mattered to him, he thought he should check on Jack.

He walked into the kitchen to find Jack sitting there with a big grin on his face. His bright purple face. His hair and clothes were also purple. The old newspapers were lying on the floor, and the kitchen table was, needless to say, very purple, as were sections of the kitchen walls and floor. Then a purple shape rushed past. It was Mildred, who used to have beautiful white patches. Now they were bright purple patches. He had no chance of catching her, as she sped off to redecorate other parts of the house. Barney realised he had to do something quickly before Alison came home. But it was too late. He heard the sound of her car pulling up outside. A few minutes later she walked into the kitchen and surveyed the scene.

Jack was still grinning.

'Hello mummy. Daddy gave me three bags of crisps.'

Alison dumped her shopping bags on the floor, turned around and stormed off upstairs without saying a word. He heard her lock herself in the bedroom. He'd be sleeping in one of the spare rooms tonight. Then he'd be shouted at in the morning. He picked up Jack, dumped him on the lawn outside and turned the garden hose on him. Jack was no longer grinning. He was now crying his eyes out. Once he was no longer purple, Barney dried him and put his pyjamas on, then sent him to bed and spent the rest of the evening cleaning the kitchen and trying to catch Mildred. It hadn't turned out to be an enjoyable Saturday after all.

On Sunday morning, Barney received a severe talking to, but it was nothing like as bad as he had been expecting. He presumed he had got of lightly because of the good job he'd made of the cleaning up. Years of working on vending machines meant he was very proficient at clearing up messes like this. The only bit he hadn't cleaned was the purple cat. He had spent much of the evening trying to catch Mildred, but she was too fast and had plenty of hiding places. She came running up to Alison straight away, and was eventually, after hours of washing and combing, restored to her natural white and grey colour.

Once he'd decided Alison has virtually forgiven him, he brought up the subject of returning to work.

'What's your plan for returning to work?' asked Barney.

'I can't go next week. I've got childcare sorted for the following week. Your mum says she would be very happy to look after him, but I don't think it would be fair on her to leave him with her for too long. I'm intending to travel down on Sunday. Would you be able come back next weekend?'

'Yes. No problem. I'll work all week, then drive home on Friday evening. I can look after Jack on Sunday.'

'Are you sure? On second thoughts, maybe I'd be better off leaving one of the cats in charge.'

Barney was silently fuming at her comment, but didn't want to show it, so refused to respond. Her jibe was uncalled for. It was just one little mishap with a bit of paint. It could have happened to anyone.

6

Barney arrived at the Vendetta office in Winchester on Monday morning. When he walked out of here five years ago, he never in his wildest dreams expected to be coming back. He'd been back once to return his car, but the idea of returning to work was beyond belief. He stood outside for a moment, then almost turned away to go back to his car. But he knew he didn't have much choice. He reluctantly entered the building and found Mary.

'Thanks so much for doing this. I really appreciate it.'

'Would you mind not being so nice? It makes me feel uneasy. How about you tell me exactly how you want me to help out?'

'There're a few outstanding jobs that I'm struggling to clear. I might need you to go along and see if you can complete them. Also, we've got two new trainee engineers, but quite frankly I'm not all that impressed with them. Would you be able to spend a day or two with them? Give them a bit of training, and give me your opinion on their competence, and if you think they have the potential to do the job.'

Barney wasn't ideally suited to the role of a mentor to new trainees. He didn't have the patience. People in general annoyed him. He usually found trainees either too full of themselves, too dumb to learn, or too eager to please and would spend all day asking pointless questions.

'Okay. That should be a laugh.'

'It's not meant to be a laugh. This is a serious situation.'

'I know. I didn't really mean it would be a laugh. I meant it would be the opposite. Don't fret. I can do serious.'

'Good. You can start that tomorrow. I have another task for you today. That idiot Liam has a problem with one of his customers. Could you meet up with him and go to sort it out.'

'Hey, that's my friend you're talking about.'

'I know. But you have to admit he is an idiot.'

'He's also your boyfriend, and the father of your child.'

'I know. And I love him. Outside of work he's good fun, a great dad, and in the bedroom ...'

'Whoa! Can I stop you there? I don't want to hear about that.'

'My point is, despite all his attributes, he's a useless engineer. He has struggled since you left as he used to rely heavily on your help. Quite frankly I don't think he'll be working at Vendetta for much longer. He's been looking at other jobs. But meanwhile, go and sort out this problem. It's at the Compleat Angler Hotel in Marlow.'

'Oh, I remember that place. It's in a beautiful location next to the Thames, a bridge, and a church. They spell 'complete' wrong. I don't know why. I believe it was mentioned in Three Men in a Boat by Jerome K. Jerome.'

'Thanks for telling me that. That's really fucking helpful.'

'My pleasure. I've been there before with Liam. He was looking for a leak, but it turned out that the river had burst its banks and the supposed leak was really the Thames coming up through the floorboards. Of course there's no way this would be the same thing, would it? Liam might not be the sharpest tool in the box, but surely he wouldn't make the same mistake twice? Although, come to think of it, there's been a lot of flooding in the news lately.'

'I don't know. Go and find out. And be on your best behaviour. No being rude or argumentative with customers. I know you don't have to worry about getting fired, but just try to be a bit more tolerant.'

'I'll try.'

'And no going to the pub either. There's too much work to be done.'

Barney knew she was wasting her breath telling him that. He hadn't seen Liam for a while, and they had a lot to catch up on. They would be definitely having a pint.

Barney drove out from the office car park and straight into a traffic jam. This was the thing Barney didn't miss at all. He hated traffic jams and hated the way other people drove their cars. In particular, he hated the ones who didn't use their indicators. It was something that took no effort to do, but whether it was through laziness, selfishness, or stupidity, so many drivers just refuse to do it. He was about to encounter such a driver.

The cause of the traffic jam was a closed lane, meaning two lanes were going into one. He was sitting in the open lane, and young lady, probably in her early twenties wanted to cut her car across in front of Barneys. He decided that if she indicated, he would let her in. If she didn't, he wouldn't. She didn't. So he kept inching forward, stopping her getting across. She blared her horn, but he wouldn't budge. Her car was getting so close to his, and they were now level with each other, and they were staring at each other face to face. He couldn't understand her mindset. It can't have been all that long since she passed her driving test. She would have failed if she had driven like this. He tried to make his point by pointing at her indicators. She responded with a hand gesture of her own. It was the traditional 'wanker' gesture. This prompted him to wind down his window and speak to her.

'It's very decent of you to offer, but I'm a bit busy right now.'

This unexpected response took her by surprise, and she had no comeback. She just stared blankly at him and gave up the fight. She stopped moving forward, then dropped her car in behind his.

Two hours later he met Liam in the Compleat Angler Hotel car park. They agreed to get the job out of the way first, then have a catch up afterwards. They reported to the reception. The receptionist called the duty manager who appeared five minutes later.

As always used to happen in the old days when they went on a job together, Barney did the talking.

'Hello, we're from Vendetta. We've come to get your vending machine working.'

'Great. It's in the staff rest room, down in the cellar. I haven't been down there to check, but our staff are saying the machine is completely dead.'

Liam followed Barney down the stairs and Barney opened the cellar door. He couldn't believe his eyes. There was a small flight of stairs down into the room, but they couldn't go down them. The whole room was flooded, and the water level was halfway up the machine. Barney turned to Liam.

'Is this how it was when you were here before.'

'Yes. Do you think it's got a leak?

Barney didn't answer that. Instead, he walked back to the reception and Liam followed. They asked to see the duty manager again. This time he took ten minutes to arrive, by which time Barney was getting agitated.

'Hello. Is the machine working now?'

'No, it isn't. The machine is half covered by the river Thames. Who knows what damage has been done? But for certain it will have blown fuses and tripped your circuit breaker.'

'Can you do anything about it?'

'Yes, I believe I can. Because I'm King Canute.'

'I realise you can't make the water subside. But can you repair the damage?'

'Yes, but I'll have to go and change into my frogman gear.'

'You don't seem to be taking this seriously. I want my machine working.'

'The machine isn't designed to work underwater. I doubt that machine will ever work again. I suggest you call us again when the water has subsided, and we can assess the damage. Then we can decide if it's repairable, or you need a new one. Meanwhile there is nothing else we can do.'

On that note they departed. But not completely. Or should that be compleat;y? Barney and Liam sat outside by the river and ordered a couple of pints. On their previous visit they were shocked at the cost of the drinks, but now money was no object for Barney, although because of old habits, he still objected to paying too much.

The drinks arrived. Barney said, 'Did you know this is the hotel where the Sunderland team stayed in 1973 when they won the FA cup at Wembley?'

'Of course I did. Even though it happened years before I was born, have no interest in football, and even less interest in Sunderland, you never forget a thing like that.'

'I'm impressed. Your sarcasm is coming along nicely. I hope you don't talk to customers like that. Actually, I hope you do.'

'Why do you support Sunderland anyway? It must be a thousand miles away. I dread to think how many miles it would be there and back.'

'Liam. If it was a thousand miles, which it isn't, there and back would be.... Well try working it out for yourself. If ever I start a quiz team, are you going to be our geography specialist? Or do you prefer maths?'

'I'm equally good at both. So why do you support them?'

'When I was a small boy, I used to sit with my dad when the football scores were read out on Grandstand. When they read out the Sunderland score, I thought they were saying Thunderland. I thought it was the coolest name out of all the teams. I always looked out for their score and was happy when they won. But little did I know, it's like a highly addictive drug. Once you support Sunderland, you can't stop. You just keep going back for more, no matter how much harm it does to you.'

They chatted for more than half an hour and had a second pint.

'How are you coping with being a dad?'

'It's a piece of cake. Louis is such a good boy. How about you?'

'If it's a piece of cake, it must be rock cake. I'm finding it somewhat harder. Jack is not such a good boy. Not for me at least. I had an incident last weekend with some purple paint. Alison blamed me, as usual. She gave me a hard time over it. But what am I supposed to do? Most kids would be happy sitting quietly colouring in a picture of a cat. My kid has to colour in the real cat instead.'

They finished their drinks and wandered back to the car park.

'What are you doing for the rest of today?'

'Mary wants me to go to Winchester railway station. They've got a snack and canned drink machine on one of the platforms that isn't working. Then I'm going back to my hotel and taking it easy. Tomorrow I'm spending the day with one of the new recruits. Someone called Kenneth.'

They went their separate ways. Barney arrived at Winchester station and sat in the car for a while. Then he eventually entered the station. He wandered along the platform towards the vending machine, but he was intercepted by an angry looking man.

'I've been waiting for forty-five minutes.'

'For a bar of chocolate? You must be desperate.'

'Are you trying to be funny?'

'No. I'm really not. Is it a bottle of coke you are desperate for?

'Have you got a problem?'

'Yes. I seem to attract strangers who ask daft questions.'

'You are really most unhelpful.'

'I would be more likely to help you if I knew what the hell you were talking about. What have you been waiting forty-five minutes for?'

'My train to London. It was due at quarter past three and its now past four o'clock.'

'Ah. Well I'm a vending machine engineer.'

'You all work for the same company.'

'No, we don't. As you can see from my badge, I work for Vendetta. We deal with vending machines. We don't have anything to do with the trains. Go and speak to one of the staff with South Western Trains on their uniform.'

The man walked away without a word. Barney shouted to him,

'That's alright. Glad to help.'

He went back to his hotel, had a hot bath, a cup of tea, and watched the Simpsons. He was just planning to relax for the rest of the evening, and maybe pop out for a walk later. He was hoping that this man Kenneth who was accompanying him tomorrow would be easy to get on with.

7

Barney had booked himself into a hotel in Winchester for the week, as he would be starting off in the depot every day. He had wandered around the city centre in the evening and found a few decent pubs. But he didn't overdo it, because he'd become used to not having to get up early in the morning, so he needed to feel reasonably healthy the next day.

He got to the office early, so popped into the canteen for a cup of tea and read his newspaper. But after ten minutes, his peace was disturbed by a stranger who came up to him and said, 'Hello. You must be Cecil.'

'Yes.'

'I'm Kenneth. Mary told me I'd find you here.'

Barney had never had any position of power during all his working years, and he wanted to show he was in charge today. So he told him to sit down while he finished his tea. He was doing this on his terms.

When he was ready, he said, 'Ok Ken. It's time to hit the road. Let's get out of here.'

'My name is Kenneth. I would prefer it if you didn't call me Ken.'

'Fair enough. As we're establishing our preferred names, I don't like being called Cecil. Everyone calls me Barney.'

'Why do you they call you Barney?'

Barney had taken an instant dislike to this bloke. He wasn't impressed that he couldn't work out that Barney was just short for Barnard. As he often did when he didn't like someone, he decided to be difficult.

'I'm named after Barney McGrew.'

'Who's Barney McGrew?'

'He was a firefighter. In a place called Trumpton. A colleague of the Pugh twins. Not to mention Cuthbert, Dibble and Grub.'

'Were you once a firefighter?'

'No. I'm a darts player. I was making that thing about the fireman up. They really named me after the five times world champion Raymond Van Barneveld. He was nicknamed Barney too.'

By now, Kenneth was confused. He'd taken an instant mutual dislike to Barney, and he was happy with that. It should make his real purpose of being here even more enjoyable.

They set off in Barney's car. The first task they had was in Newbury, which wasn't too long a drive, but seemed like hours because the two of them weren't keen on talking to each other. The reported fault was a snack machine that was completely dead. On first inspection Barney found a blown fuse. Luckily, he had a packet of ten fuses in the back of his car. He collected the fuses and explained to Kenneth what he was going to do. The first step would be to change the fuse and see if the new one blew. He put the fuse in and it blew immediately. But before he could take the next step, Action by Def Leppard interrupted him. The screen displayed Sweary.

'Sorry to disturb you. One of the other new trainees is out on his own for the first time. He's encountered a problem he can't resolve. Would you mind talking to him on the phone and see if you can help him out?'

'Yeah, okay. Tell him to call me.'

The trainee called him and explained his predicament. Barney had to go back to the car yet again to get a circuit diagram. He told Kenneth to wait next to the machine. The phone call took just over ten minutes, but he successfully helped solve the problem. Then he returned to the machine, and Kenneth.

'Sorry about that. Now the next step is to disconnect some of the parts that might be causing the fuse to blow. Then put in another new fuse. It's kind of a process of elimination. But I assume you must know stuff like this.'

'Have you got any more fuses?'

'Yes. There's a packet of ten. Or nine now.'

'No. They're all blown.'

'They aren't blown. It's a new packet.'

'I tried them all when you were on the phone. And now they're all blown.'

'Tell me this is a wind up.'

'No. I'm telling you the truth.'

'Are you trying to tell me you kept putting in fuses one after the other without disconnecting anything, until they were all blown? And now I don't have any left to finish the job?'

'Yes.'

'Give me strength.'

'I was only doing what you did.'

'I did it once to prove something. You did it repeatedly for no useful purpose, and wasted all my fuses in the process.'

'How was I supposed to know that?'

Barney paused and took a deep breath.

'How much engineering experience have you had?'

'Not a lot.'

'Could you be more specific?'

'None.'

'Yet you are intending to do the job of an engineer?'

'How hard can it be? Besides, I've heard that vending machines are just computers these days, and I'm a wizard with computers.'

'Some of them can have unnecessarily complicated programming, but you still need to be able to do the nuts and bolts stuff. Quite frankly, if you think it's going to be so easy, you're going to be in for a bit of a shock.'

They arrived at their next assignment, and Barney knew he would have to do the work while Kenneth watched. He was so pissed off with Kenneth that he was going to do his best to make him look stupid.

He had to fit a new heater element to a boiler, and there was no way he was going to trust him to do it. Not after the fiasco with the fuses. He had to stand on a chair to change the element from above, and he needed Kenneth to pass up tools to him.

'Pass me the Phillips head screwdriver.'

Kenneth fumbled around in the tool bag for a while before Barney, by now growing impatient said, 'It's the one with the blue handle.'

Kenneth found the screwdriver and passed it to him. Ten minutes later Barney asked him to find an adjustable spanner. Much to Barney's disappointment, Kenneth got lucky and found the spanner at the first attempt. But Barney wasn't about to let him off the hook easily. He wanted to test him further.

'No, not that one, I need a metric one,'

Kenneth went back to the tool bag for another look. He fumbled around for a while, but clearly didn't have a clue what he was looking for.

'It's alright', said Barney, 'That one will do just fine.'

The rest of the day dragged slowly over. They did another three calls, but Barney already knew Kenneth wasn't up to the job, and Kenneth didn't want the job anyway. They eventually drove back to Winchester and returned to the canteen. Liam was in the canteen drinking coffee and playing a game on his phone, waiting for Mary to finish work so they could go home together. Barney left Kenneth with Liam while he reported to Mary.

'Hi, I'm Liam. How did you get on today?'

'Not too bad. But I don't think Cecil likes me very much.'

'Oh, don't worry about him. He doesn't like anybody very much. Besides, you won't have to see him for much longer. He's only working here for another week or two.'

'Really? Why is that?'

'He has already retired. He only came back to help out for a few weeks. He won the lottery a few years ago. He's a millionaire.'

'Is he now?… Is he just?'

Meanwhile Barney had found Mary.

'Sorry Mary but the man is useless. As an engineer, he makes Liam look like Isambard Kingdom Brunel.'

'Hey, that's my boyfriend you're talking about.'

'Let's not do all that again. But seriously. My recommendation is that you don't employ him. Not only is he technically inept. He's a pain in the arse too. I'm glad I won't have to deal with him again.'

'Fair enough. Thanks for doing that anyway. I'll tell him to take a hike.'

But she didn't get the chance. Kenneth had already left the building. His real purpose here had been served.

8

Barney reported for duty early on Wednesday morning. He was waiting for Mary to finish a phone call, so he had a cup of tea and did the crossword in his newspaper. The phone call ended, and he asked her what she wanted him to do today. But before she could tell him, the phone rang again. She answered it.

'Good morning. You are through to Vendetta. How may I help you?'

'Good morning. I am calling because I'm having a few problems with my coffee machine.'

'Oh, I'm terribly sorry to hear that. What seems to be the problem?'

'When I press for a drink, the wrong drink comes out.'

'Oh dear. My apologies for that. I think the best course of action would be for me to pass the information to one of our engineers and he will be with you as soon as possible.'

'Thank you so much. You have been very helpful.'

'My pleasure. Is there anything else I can help you with?'

'No. That will be all thank you.'

'Thank you. Have a nice day.'

Mary ended the call while Barney made a fake retching noise in the background. She decided he would be the engineer she would pass the information to. She switched from talking to a customer mode to talking to an engineer mode.

'Hey, numb nuts. This stupid prick can't work his coffee machine. Get your arse over there and sort him out. If it's not too much fucking trouble.'

'Of course, ma'am. Only too pleased to help. It'll be my pleasure. Would you like me to kiss your feet? Have a nice day.'

'You can kiss my arse. Then when you've sorted out that one, would you pop over to Basingstoke? A customer is complaining that the lightbulb in their machine isn't working and they want it fixed immediately.'

'Is that why you wanted me back? To change a light bulb. Why don't you send one of the new trainees? Even Kenneth could probably manage to fit a new light bulb.'

'Kenneth didn't come in today. I don't think we'll be seeing him again. Spending a day with you has clearly frightened him off. You'll be passing through Basingstoke on your way back from the other job. It makes sense for you to do it.'

'Since when has making sense been part of this job?'

Barney went to the first job and solved it in a few minutes. They were getting the wrong drinks because someone had filled the sugar cannister with chocolate powder. Then he drove to Basingstoke to deal with the light bulb crisis. He expected this one to be an easy fix too. But it didn't turn out that way. There were some new machines that weren't around when he last worked. It wasn't one he was familiar with.

He took a replacement light tube to the machine and swapped it. But much to his surprise, the new one didn't come on either. On further investigation he found a converter board that powered the light tube. Someone had unplugged it. He had no idea who had done it, or why, but was fairly certain that was the reason for the lack of illumination. He plugged the board in. Still the light didn't come on. By now he was getting a little frustrated. He should know by now it was a mistake to assume a job would be quick and easy.

The only logical conclusion was that the board was faulty, so he went back to the car to see if he had a spare one among the box of junk he'd been given on Monday. Luckily, he did. He grabbed the board and returned to the building. But something was wrong. There were crowds of people outside the office, and when he tried to enter the building, a security guard told him he couldn't come in.

'Sorry mate. The fire alarms have gone off. We didn't have a drill scheduled, so we're investigating at the moment. It may be a while before we can go back in.'

Barney cursed his luck. He also cursed whichever idiot caused the fire alarms to go off. He had to stand outside for almost half an hour before the crowds started to go back inside the building. He waited until everyone else had gone in, then wandered in. The security guard stopped him again.

'We've found the reason for the fire alarms going off. There was smoke billowing out of the vending machine. The same vending machine you were working on. Not only did the alarms go off, but the sprinklers were activated too. It's rather soggy up there.'

He returned to the machine and found that the smoke had been coming from the board he'd plugged in. It was completely burnt out now. He fitted the new board, and much to his relief the light came on. He packed up his tools and got away from there as quickly as he could. Meanwhile, unknown to Barney, someone had phoned the Vendetta office to make a complaint, and said they would be demanding financial compensation as soon as the cost of any damage was established.

He returned to the office, but when he walked in, he was greeted with loud cheers and mocking laughter.

'Ooh look out everybody. It's the fire starter.'

'Hey, Barney McGrew! You're meant to put fires out, not cause them.'

Then the whole office all chanted in harmony the immortal rhyme, 'Pugh, Pugh, Barney McGrew, Cuthbert, Dibble and Grub.'

Mary felt the need to have a go herself. 'You prat. Can't I trust you to do a simple task like changing a light bulb, without burning down the building?'

By now, Barney was getting a bit pissed off. 'That's the last time I do any favours for you. Next time get some other mug to help you out, And I didn't burn down the building. There was just a bit of smoke. And that wouldn't have happened if the previous engineer to go there had done his job properly instead of just unplugging the board and leaving it like that without telling anybody.'

But Mary was enjoying herself too much to care.

'Oh, don't be like that. If it's any consolation, I'll be telling Richard Bowles all about it when I visit him in hospital tomorrow. That should cheer him up a bit.'

Later that evening, Barney was in the hotel bar and called Alison. They discussed their plans for the weekend and the following week.

He told her, 'I'm planning on coming home on Friday evening, then returning on Monday morning for one more week. Mum is going to look after Jack for the week.'

'I hope she makes a better job of it than you did.'

'Will you ever let me forget it?'

'I'll never mention it again.'

'How is the little… rascal?'

'Fine. I took him to the hairdressers today.'

'What? I thought you liked his hair the way it was Did they cut it all off?'

Alison was very proud of Jack's blonde curly hair.

'No, of course not. I just wanted them to tidy it up a bit. Especially after all the times I washed it to get rid of the purple paint.'

'Well done. You managed to go at least two minutes before mentioning it again. What are your plans for next week?'

'I'm travelling down on Sunday afternoon. Mary and I are going out for a drink and catch up on Sunday evening. Then I'm going to work on Monday and see how I can help her out.'

'In that case I'll see you on Friday, then maybe we can go somewhere with Jack on Saturday.'

'Ok. See you on Friday.'

Barney finished his pint and went back to his room.

9

Barney had no intention of doing much work today. The events of yesterday had left him wishing he hadn't bothered coming back to work. He was determined to make next week his final contribution, no matter how much Mary pleaded, and no matter how much Alison insisted. He was staying in a London hotel this evening. His darts team had a match, and he was taking the opportunity to see his old friends again. He had seen them occasionally since their lottery win, but tonight he had the chance to play for the team once more.

He intended finishing work early. But first he had been sent to Staines Magistrates Court to look at a machine that had been reported as vandalised. This raised a few questions in Barney's head. He'd been to this machine before. It was situated in a large room where various lowlifes of society, and a few unfortunate victims of society were being briefed by their solicitors before going into court. He had no doubt there were plenty of them capable of vandalising a vending machine. But was it such a wise thing to do?

'I've got an hour to wait for my trial. How can I amuse myself while I'm waiting to convince the magistrates I'm fundamentally a good, but misunderstood person and if they go easy on me today, I'll never do anything wrong ever again? I know. I'll commit an act of wanton vandalism in a building full of police and magistrates and solicitors.'

He hadn't seen Mary today. She wasn't in the office. She was visiting Richard Bowles in hospital. Bowles was Barney's old boss. They didn't get on very well. For years Bowles had dealt with complaints from customers about Barney's attitude. They have had many arguments over the years. Bowles was generally much happier since Barney had retired, but it would appear that the years of stress had taken their toll. He was now quite ill in hospital. He felt a bit sorry for him, and hoped that he hadn't contributed in any way to his condition.

Mary arrived at the hospital and was greeted by Richard Bowles's wife.

'Thanks for coming Mary. I think he needs to see someone else. He's fed up with me, and just gets worked up and criticises me.'

'It's no problem. Glad to help.'

'I've got to warn you, he's under the influence of various drugs they've been giving him. He sometimes forgets where he is, and who he's talking to. He might talk a lot of nonsense.'

Mary resisted the temptation of saying he sounded just like his old self. It might not have gone down well with his wife. They walked into the room where Bowles was lying. He was wired up to a machine with flashing lights and lots of bleeping.

His wife said, 'Hello dear. You have a visitor. It's Mary from work.'

'Hi Richard', said Mary.

Fortunately, he did recognise her.

'Hello Mary. It's so good of you to come. I'm sorry to have left you in charge.'

'Thanks very much.'

'No, I didn't mean it like that. I meant sorry for leaving it all to you. I'm still not saying it right, am I? But I'm sorry all the same. How's the company doing in my absence? Is everything running smoothly?'

'No, not really. There have been quite a few problems.'

Mary didn't know if she was just imagining it, but she thought some of the flashing lights on the machine he was connected to were getting faster, and the bleeps were getting louder.

'Problems. What sort of problems?'

'I didn't want to have to tell you this one, but I'll have to because you are going to have to deal with it when you come back. There was a complaint about Barney, and we're going to get a bill for some damage.'

He'd heard words like this before. But he wasn't convinced he was hearing them now.

'Barney? Are you winding me up? The only Barney I know is Cecil Barnard. He doesn't even work for us any longer. I thought we had managed to get rid of him four years ago. I must be hallucinating. Am I dreaming? Or more accurately having a nightmare?'

'No. He came back to work to help me out. I was desperate, and he is a good engineer, despite what you think of him.'

By now the flashing lights and bleeps were definitely getting faster and louder.

'Why the hell would you do that? Have you taken leave of your senses?'

'I hope not. Just calm down.'

'Don't tell me to calm down. How do you expect me to calm

down? What did he do? Tell me what he did.'

'Nothing too bad. He caused a building to be evacuated and set off some sprinklers which caused some damage. So they say.'

This tipped Bowles over the edge. He shouted at the top of his voice, 'Nurse! Nurse! Help!'

The nurse came running and tried to calm him down. But she failed.

'That woman is mad! She's trying to kill me! She's trying to kill me! Get her out of here!'

Bowles wife led Mary, who was visibly shaken, out of the room.

'Don't take it personally Mary. I warned you he wasn't himself. He'll be all right. Thanks for coming.'

Barney checked into his hotel in the Kensington area of west London. It wasn't the best choice of location for someone so reluctant to part with his ample supply of money. But he wanted somewhere that wasn't too difficult to get back to after a probably heavy night at the darts. He just took it easy for the afternoon. He couldn't be bothered to go out anywhere and just lay on his bed playing games on his phone. At six o'clock he got the tube to Moorgate. As the train was travelling between Edgware Road and Baker Street stations, a recorded voice came over the loudspeaker.

'The next station is Baker Street. Alight here for Madame Tussauds.'

Barney couldn't see the point of this announcement. Surely if somebody was visiting Madame Tussauds, they would check first which station it was near. They wouldn't just get on a random train and travel around all day, waiting for an announcement to tell them it was time to get off. That sort of thing wound him up. And he was wound up again five minutes later when another announcement told him to alight at Euston Square station for the British Library. He wondered if these places were even open at this time of day. He quickly googled Madame Tussauds opening times on his phone and discovered that they closed at 15.00 and would reopen at 10.00 the next morning. Therefore, the announcement was doubly pointless. The other thing that he often heard over the loudspeaker on his tube journeys was 'Please make sure you have all your belongings with you'.

'That's not possible. How am I supposed to bring all my belongings with me on a train journey? Do I have to go home and bring everything from my house? And how would I get my car down here?'

He imagined another announcement in his head.

'The next station is Moorgate. Alight here for the Black Cat. And don't leave your darts on the train, you moron.'

His fantasising helped him pass the journey, and before long he was in the Black Cat, the pub where his team the Mickey Mouse Club played their home games. Just as it always used to be, Tom and Daffy were already in the pub, having a good pre-match drink. Roy, Fiona, and Joe all turned up in the following half hour. They had recruited a new player to replace Barney, who couldn't travel from the Lake District for games, but as luck would have it, he wasn't available this evening, so Barney was back in the team. Roy would have found a place in the team for him anyway.

They were playing their old rivals Norfolk and Good (the name that sounds like a firm of solicitors, but when said out loud takes on a completely different meaning) so they were expecting a lively evening with a lot of drinking. And that was how it turned out.

The team were all real ale drinkers apart from Barney who was the only lager drinker, and Fiona who generally drank white wine. But tonight, Daffy was also on wine, which surprised everyone. When it came to Fiona's round, she asked Daffy what he would like.

'What would you like to drink, Mr Duck? The usual? A pint of Old Sheepdip?'

'You know fine well it's called Old Sheepdog. And no. I would not like to have the usual. This evening I'm on the Cabernet Sauvignon. A large one please If that's not too much trouble.'

'There must be something wrong with my ears. For a moment it sounded like you asked for Cabernet Sauvignon. As if you'd know what that was.'

'Very funny. For your information, I'm on the red wine tonight.'

'Why? Are you feeling alright? Perhaps you need to lie down for a while.'

'I'm feeling fine thank you, Nurse Fiona. However, now that you mention it, I did have a visit to the doctors last week and she told me I had high blood pressure and am a little overweight.'

'So, you thought you'd rectify that by getting pissed on red wine instead of beer?'

'Exactly. I'm sure I read something recently experts say if you drink a bottle of red wine every day it protects you against heart disease due to high levels of antioxidants.'

'That's a glass of red wine a day, not a bottle, you fuckwit.'

'And you are obviously so clever. What do you think a bottle is made of?'

'What the container is made of is irrelevant. It's the amount I'm talking about. A bottle contains about four or five glasses.'

'There you go then. If one glass a day is good for you, just think how good a whole bottle is.'

'Yes. Have you ever thought of visiting planet Earth sometime? I hear it's quite nice at this time of year.'

Barney sat and listened to this incredible conversation and was laughing his head off. How he'd missed these people. He was content with life in the Lake District, but the only downside was most of his friends were in the south and he didn't see them so much.

Barney didn't play very well. He hadn't played for a while and was hopelessly out of practice. It came as no surprise when he lost all of his games. But he still had a great time, and the team of now millionaires had some interesting tales to tell. They also took the opportunity to arrange the next annual excursion. They had been to Dublin the previous year, which was predictably a very drunken affair and also managed to include a darts match in which they took a severe thrashing after coming up against a team which played in a league way above their usual standard. Roy had suggested Cornwall for the next one. He'd been in touch with a team from Penzance who were keen to give them a game, which would be followed by a couple of days enjoying the scenery and local culture with the occasional pub visit thrown in. He would have to tell Alison. She had been on the Dublin trip and had a great time, but, didn't usually go with them on these mini tours, and was unlikely to want to go to Cornwall. At least he hoped not. It wasn't that he would behave any different if she was there, it was just that it would be less stressful if he didn't have to worry whether she was enjoying herself. He headed back to his hotel feeling happy. He had something to look forward to.

10

Friday morning had arrived. Barney was feeling exactly how he used to feel every Friday morning after a darts night. It had been a long week and working again had been tough. He didn't want to do it again. He had promised Mary one more week, then he was going to retire yet again and get back to his tranquil life in the Lake District. With his bossy wife, out of control son, a cat which tolerated him, and another cat which hated him. Maybe not quite as tranquil as he'd wished for, although it was a nice life all the same. But first he had to get through today.

Mary had sent him a job to go to Reading, but on his screen the machine fault was just described as 'unknown problem'. Then following that she wanted him to meet Liam at Heston services on the M4 to help him with an installation at the Travelodge. He looked up 'Sweary' on his phone and called the number.

'What exactly do you mean by unknown problem? And how can I be expected to repair the machine if I don't know what is supposed to wrong with it?'

Mary didn't have much more information to offer.

'How the fuck should I know?'

She was in a bad mood following her encounter with Richard Bowles yesterday. And she partly blamed Barney. It was the news of his antics that had sent Bowles over the edge.

'I received an Email from head office. I'll tell you exactly what is says, and you will have to work it out for yourself. It says unknown problem, customer is not happy. Machine gone. And that's where it ends. I am guessing the end of the sentence is missing. It should probably be machine gone wrong, or machine gone crazy or something like that. Just go there and solve it. I'm not in the mood to be hassled.'

Barney was used to Mary's abrasive character, but she'd was extra tetchy this morning. He thought she might act overly nice to him because he was doing her such a big favour, but he needn't have worried. He could have done without this one. He was going to face an irate customer while nursing a hangover. Not a great combination, although one that he should have been used to by now. He reluctantly drove to Reading. On arrival, a receptionist called the site contact, who came to the reception and introduced himself. Barney's initial assessment of him was that he was either in a very bad mood, or he was just permanently horrible. In comparison to him, Mary was Mother Theresa. He didn't have to tolerate any abuse. He could just tell the man to get stuffed and walk out. He could even fulfil one of his dreams of throwing a cup of coffee in someone's face. Or just chop the mains cable off the machine and tell the customer the machine is unsafe to use, quoting a string of made up health and safety regulations, and had to be rendered unusable. But he had lost some of his confrontational nature in the four years since his retirement. In other words, he just couldn't be bothered any more. But this one would put him to the test.

'What the hell is wrong with your company?'

'Quite a few things. But can you be more specific?'

'Everyone I have tried to talk to on the phone doesn't appear to have a clue what they're talking about. Does your company only employ stupid people?'

'They employ me. Are you implying that I'm stupid too?'

'That remains to be seen.'

The Barney from a few years ago would have laid into him for that. But he remained calm.

'How about you show me to the machine, and I can prove I'm not stupid by repairing your machine?'

'Are you trying to be funny?'

'No. I'm being deadly serious. Take me to the machine and we can get this over with.'

'Did you not get my Email?'

'Yes. But it was somewhat lacking in clarity. It just said machine gone.'

'That sounds pretty clear to me. The machine has gone.'

'Gone where?'

'I don't know. I came in this morning, and it wasn't there anymore.'

'I see. And where do I fit in?'

'Good God. It would be quicker to train a chimp.'

If Barney had the cup of coffee in his hand, that would have been the moment. He just about managed to keep his cool. At least on the outside.

'Would you like to take me to the place where the machine used to be?'

He was led to the space where the machine once stood. Barney took a magnifying glass out of his toolbox and did a Sherlock Holmes impression, scanning the empty space with the magnifying glass while mumbling things like 'Aha' or 'Interesting', and even finished off with 'Elementary my dear Watson.'

He turned to the man and said, 'I have completed my investigation, and there can only be one conclusion.'

'And what would that be?'

'That you are a knobhead.'

'How dare you? You can't speak to me like that.'

'I can, and I just did. Not only do you expect me to locate a machine that isn't there anymore, but you are an obnoxious git, and horrible to people who haven't done anything to deserve it. People who are just trying to do their jobs. Now I'm leaving, and with a bit of luck I will never see you again,'

Barney walked back to his car feeling good. It reminded him of the feeling he had four years ago after he had told an even more obnoxious customer to shove his cock in a cup of hot coffee in order to prove it wasn't hot enough. Back then it would have cost him his job, if he hadn't resigned first, but he had no such worries now. He was glad to get out of there and headed off to meet Liam. It would be a good tale to tell while they were drinking their usual pint.

Barney and Liam were an odd pair. They had been friends for a few years, but didn't have much in common. When they were single, they would go to nightclubs. Liam was tall and good looking, and had the knack of attracting girls. He always got the best one and Barney was often left with her less attractive mate, or more often than not left with nobody. They would go to the pub after, and sometimes during work. The conversation usually involved Barney getting annoyed at Liam because he was being stupid, or Liam getting annoyed because Barney was treating him like he was stupid. There had been more than one occasion when Liam had come very close to thumping Barney when he had wound him up a bit too far, but had just about managed to restrain himself. He was physically stronger and did karate lessons. But they had remained friends, and now their nightclubbing days were over, or at least the pursuit of girls element of it was over. They both were now in relationships and had a son each.

Heston service station was on the M4 just west of London. It didn't take him long to get there from Reading. He was slightly later than the arranged meeting time, but when he arrived at the reception there was no sign of Liam. He called him.

'Are you going to be much longer? I'm at the hotel reception now?'

'I'm at the hotel reception too, I can't see you.'

They both wandered around but couldn't find each other.

Liam asked, 'You are on the westbound side, aren't you?'

'No. It clearly says eastbound on the job.'

'Yes, it always says eastbound whenever I get sent here, but it should say westbound.'

'Don't you think that was worth mentioning?'

'With hindsight, yes, it probably was.'

Liam stood on a bench and waved. Barney could see him. It would take him two minutes to walk to him if you were allowed to walk across the M4.

'Yes, I can see you. How do I get over there? There's no bridge.'

'You'll have to drive to the next junction at Brentford, then back again. It's about ten miles altogether.'

Barney's euphoric feeling had disappeared. Much to his surprise, Liam's estimate of the distance was pretty accurate, but it took 45 minutes due to heavy traffic at the Brentford junction.

'What kept you?'

'I was delayed because some imbecile forgot to tell me that when they said, eastbound they actually meant westbound. What do you need help with?'

'Nothing. I've already done the job. It was a straightforward machine swap.'

'Why the hell did Sweary send me here then? She was in a right mood this morning.'

'Hey, that's my girlfriend you're talking about.'

'Don't you start all that. I get the same from her every time I make a derogatory remark about you. You're happy the job is definitely done? Properly?'

'Yes. The customer isn't happy though. He insists that the drinks don't taste right, even though it's exactly the same machine with exactly the same ingredients. There's just no pleasing some people. Hold on a minute. What did you just say?'

'Nothing. Just joking. I've had someone like that today too. Come on. I'll tell you about it over a pint. I can't have much though. I'm driving to the Lake District afterwards.'

But Liam had taken offence.

'The reason she is in a bad mood is because Richard Bowles had a right go at her yesterday when she was at the hospital. Hearing that you were back triggered him off. Especially when she told him about your cock up with the smoking machine.'

'I didn't make a cock up. It was the engineer who visited the machine before me that made the cock up. I hope she's okay. Come on. I'll buy you a pint.'

They had to drive up the motorway and got off at the next junction where they found a decent pub and ordered two pints.

Barney told him, 'I've just driven on the smart motorway from Reading. I was driving on it for years while they were doing all the roadworks, and now they've finally finished it, I won't get a chance to use it.'

'What's a smart motorway?'

'Haven't you heard of them?'

'No. Is this another one of your wind-ups? If it is, then don't bother. I'm not in the mood.'

'No. It's not a wind up. It's a real thing. You must have heard of them.'

'No. I haven't.'

'Have you been living in a cave? On Mars? With your fingers in your ears? And your hands over your eyes?'

'No, I haven't. How can I have my fingers in my ears and my hands over my eyes at the same time?'

'Because Martians have four arms.'

'Okay. I'll play along with your silly game. Tell me about the smarty pants motorway.'

'I'm not playing any silly game. Smart motorways are a real thing. They are really good. For instance, supposing there is heavy traffic, and everyone is trundling along at 30mph, the smart motorway detects this and automatically sets the speed limit to something like 50mph so you don't drive too fast, even though you can't.'

Liam was in an uncharacteristically snappy mood.

'It doesn't sound very smart to me. It sounds like a dumb motorway. What else does it do?'

'Here's the really clever bit. They've done away with the hard shoulder. So if your car breaks down, you're stuck on the main carriageway amongst all the moving traffic instead of the hard shoulder.'

'I'm beginning to think this smart motorway should be called a thick as pig shit motorway.'

'Now, now. Liam. Some of the finest brains in the country have devised this wonderful system. Who are we to tell them it was a bad idea?'

'But what's the purpose of them though?'

'To reduce fatal accidents.'

'And has it?'

'No. Statistics show they have increased.'

'They don't sound like a good idea to me. I drive carefully anyway. I've never even had a ticket for speeding. Have you?'

Barney suspected Liam was having a dig at him. He knew fine

well Barney had been caught on speed cameras before. But he didn't take the bait.

'Yes. I've had quite a few, although not too many lately. I've learned my lesson. I've almost been banned twice. I got away with it by taking speed awareness courses. I've done three in total.'

'Were they useful?'

'Yes. They were useful in helping me avoid a ban.'

'I mean did you learn anything?'

'Yes. I learned that speed cameras are triggered at ten percent over the speed limit plus two miles per hour. For instance, if the speed limit is 30 mph, the cameras get you if you do 35. If you're on a motorway, they go off at 79 mph.'

'Right. You're telling me the only useful thing you learned was how to break the speed limit and get away with it. Doesn't that defeat the purpose?'

'Not to me. My purpose was to avoid getting any more fines and penalty points on my driving licence. It helped in that respect. Most of the other things they tried to teach us were just obvious, and the people in charge of the course were taking the moral high ground, trying to shame everyone. It was hard to concentrate. There is always some prat who won't stop asking stupid questions, usually a taxi driver or a lorry driver and there's always another one trying to impress the geezer running the course. A bit like a Vendetta training course.'

'They can't do much good if you got more speeding tickets and had to go back for more courses.'

Barney didn't like that comment. This time he reacted.

'There's nothing wrong with my driving. I've never caused a crash in the thirty-two years I've been driving. Most of the real bad drivers out there don't ever get caught. The authorities are just lazy. It's so much easier to catch drivers who go over the speed limit. Why don't they have Driving in The Fog or Rain Without Putting Your Lights On Awareness Courses? Or Pulling Across in Front of Someone Without Using Your Fucking Indicators Awareness Courses? There should be special awareness courses for anyone who puts a Baby on Board sign in their car window, to make them aware that they are a twat. And why don't they make all cyclists pass an intelligence test before they are allowed on the road? That would get rid of most of them.'

This time it was Liam's turn to bite his tongue. He cycled himself sometimes and had often had to endure Barney's rants about cyclists, which were sometimes justified, and sometimes not. But Barney was now on the warpath.

'And another thing. Why do they manufacture cars that can easily reach speeds of over a hundred miles per hour? You get treated like you're worse than Jack the Ripper if you break the speed limit. But what about the people who build the cars? If they built cars that could only do seventy, nobody would drive at eighty or ninety. It's ridiculous. I'll probably have to explain it to the Alien, once I've got it to understood about the way human beings react to haircuts, getting hit by a cricket ball in the nuts, and why farting makes you more of a man.'

'Alien? What the hell are you talking about?'

'I'll let you in to a little secret. One day I'm going to be visited by an alien. And it's going to ask me some tricky questions about the human race. But don't tell anyone.'

'Don't worry. I won't. And I think you'd better not have any more to drink.'

Liam went quiet for a while. Then he came up with another driving related comment. At first, Barney thought he was being dumb again, but it turned out he was showing rare signs of intelligence.

'You know what I can't understand? That sign with the red triangle with the aeroplane in the middle.'

'It means beware of low flying aircraft.'

'I know what it fucking means. But what's the point in them? The aeroplanes aren't going to be flying so low that they land on the top of your car. And even if they did, you couldn't do much about it.'

'Liam, I'm impressed. You have a point. I have had similar thoughts about the falling rocks warning sign. We get quite a few of those in the Lake District. I've often wondered what you are supposed to do when you see one. Do you stop, turn around and go back? Or do you drive on and take a chance that no rocks are due to fall? And likewise with the aeroplanes, if the rocks fall and land on your car, there's nothing much you can do to prevent it.'

Liam wanted to take advantage that he was saying something that was getting respected. He continued his criticism of road signs.

'I saw another road sign the other day which I also thought was a bit unnecessary. It said Street Lighting Turned Off.'

'I see. And why do you think that was unnecessary?'

'If the lights are turned off, surely you can see that for yourself.

Nobody is going to read that sign and go Ooh, I never noticed the lights weren't on. And even if they did, what difference does it make? You're not going to do anything different, are you?'

'I agree. You appear to have your finger on the pulse when it comes to road signs. If ever you get on Mastermind, it should be your specialist subject.'

Barney was becoming bored with the conversation, but Liam wasn't about to stop.

'And another thing. I don't like the signs that say Thank You for Driving Carefully Through Our Village.'

'Sigh. Why not.'

'It's a bit presumptuous. How do they know you've driven carefully through their village? Plenty of people don't drive carefully.'

'Okay. Enough with the road signs. I think we've covered it. We'll agree there are some daft ones.'

They blabbed on for a while longer about various other things, then they finished their drinks and Barney set off on the long journey home. He had a feeling Liam wasn't all that happy with him. He wondered if he had said something to offend him. One thing he was certain of was how relieved he was that the week was finally over.

11

At first glance, Liam and Mary came across as a mismatched couple. Most of their friends and work colleagues were surprised when they first got together, and were even more surprised when they stayed together and had a child.

Liam had always been successful with girls. What he lacked in brains, he made up for in good looks. Mary wasn't so blessed in that department. In fact, Liam had revealed to Barney that he wanted to ask her out before he had even met her. His attraction to her all came about from telephone conversations they had at work. He liked her voice. Then when he finally met her at the work Christmas party, they ended up in bed together at Barney's house and have been together ever since. Mary was fond of his shortcomings in the intelligence department. She liked to be in charge, and relished being the clever one. Liam didn't mind that. After years of casual relationships and meaningless one night stands, he was glad to have someone to look after him. Mary switched off her abrasive 'sweary' personality when she was at home. It was a hard act for her to keep up, and as a result she was extremely kind to Liam. It worked very well, and in sharp contrast to Alison and Barney, the two of them rarely argued about anything.

Liam collected Mary from the office and collected Louis from his nursery. Then they drove home. Mary was in a lot better mood. She was another one who was glad the week was over. But she sensed Liam had something on his mind, which was unusual in itself, because he rarely had anything on his mind.

He sat in silence for most of the journey and stared out of the window. She couldn't bear it any longer and broke the silence.

'Are you okay hun?'

'Yeah, I'm fine.'

'But?'

'But nothing.'

'Come on. Out with it.'

'Okay. It's nothing really. It's just something Barney said to me. Does he make degrog… dregog… insulting comments to you about me?'

'What sort of comments?'

'The sort of comments which suggest he thinks I'm stupid.'

'No, not at all,' she lied.

'I think he does. He virtually admitted it.'

'No, you've got it all wrong. Only just the other day he was comparing you to Isambard Kingdom Brunel.'

'What, you mean the geezer on Game of Thrones?'

'You're not really helping your case. He's not a geezer from Game of Thrones.'

'Who is he then?'

'He was… He… Erm… He was some sort of scientist. I think he built a bridge or a train or something. But I know he was really clever.'

'Oh. That's not so bad then.'

'Don't take it personally. They are good friends to us, and I'm so grateful they are helping me. They didn't need to. I'm looking forward to seeing Alison again. We're having a night out in London on Sunday. And I know Barney can be a narky sod, but his heart is in the right place. I think. And don't forget he gave us ten thousand pounds each when he won the lottery.'

'I suppose so. That did come in handy.'

'Besides, money isn't everything. I think we got the easier deal when it comes to our kids. It sounds as if they have a much harder time with Jack than we do with Louis.'

'Maybe. Sorry, it's just I'm not happy at work. I had to deal with a real dick today. I installed a machine which worked perfectly. But he insisted the drinks tasted horrible. I transferred the ingredients from the old machine. The amount of coffee beans and tea leaves and sugar and milk were programmed exactly the same as the old machine. The water shots were the same. The temperature was set exactly the same. The drinks tasted perfectly good, but he wasn't having any of it. What can you do?'

They pulled up outside their house and got out of the car.

'Just forget all about it and we'll enjoy the weekend.'

'No. I won't forget all about it. I've had enough. When I was at the gym yesterday evening, I saw on a notice board they were looking for new staff. I am thinking of applying.'

'That's fine by me, if that's what you really want. But it's not a good time for us to be losing another engineer,'

'Come off it. We all know I'm hardly the greatest engineer in the world. I'm certainly no Izzabart Kingston Broomhead. The company will survive without me. As someone once said to me, I'm not the sharpest tool in the picnic basket. Or something like that.'

She hugged him and smiled.

'Hey. That's my boyfriend you're talking about.'

12

Barney woke up on Saturday morning feeling exhausted. It had been a long and slow drive on Friday evening. Unfortunately for him, Alison wanted to make the most of the day before heading south on Sunday. On the other hand, if he was made to go out somewhere, he wouldn't be missing much in the way of sport. The Sunderland game had been switched to Sunday in order to be shown live on television. By then Alison would be gone, so hopefully he could watch it in peace, so long as Jack behaved. They opted for a walk in the countryside, followed by a pub meal. They chose a pub which was child friendly. In other words, there was an area where they could dump Jack with lots of other kids where he could run, climb, swing, slide, and shout his head off, while they could sit and have a few drinks.

Alison asked, 'What are your plans for next week?'

I'm not going on Monday. I've already told Mary I'll go on Tuesday, stay until Friday, then that's all I'm doing,'

'Was she okay with that?'

'Not really. It didn't help that Liam is off on some training course on Monday. She'll just have to like it or lump it. They're a bunch of ungrateful bastards anyway. Just look at the reaction of Richard Bowles when he heard I was helping out. And they all had a good laugh at me for setting off the fire alarms, which wasn't my fault. And they're not even paying me.'

'You are a grumpy git at times. I'm really looking forward to it.

I've checked in to a quite nice little hotel tomorrow night. Mary is coming to meet me in the afternoon. We're booked in to the spa for a bit of pampering, then we're going out in the West End for a nice meal, or maybe some dancing.'

'Oh yes. And what's this quite nice little hotel called?'

'I can't remember.'

'Don't give me that. You know fine well what it's called.'

'I believe it's called the Dorchester, or something like that.'

Barney wasn't all that happy hearing this, but wasn't shocked. Despite his wealth, he had been using Travelodge and Premier Inn during his return to work. Alison had other ideas. He knew there was no point in arguing about it.

'Can I trust you to look after Jack this time?'

'You never let up, do you? We'll be fine. I'll just keep him away from the paints.'

'And don't forget to feed the cats.'

'I won't. I thought I'd try them with some rat poison.'

'That's a horrible thing to say.'

They finished their food and collected jack from the kids play area, then had a long walk home, with a backdrop of beautiful scenery. They walked past a picturesque churchyard where there was a small group of people playing musical instruments and handing out leaflets.

Churches such as this gave Barney conflicting thoughts. He thought some of the buildings were fantastic. A church was essential to the landscape of a beautiful village such as the one where they lived. He even enjoyed walking around church graveyards, which he thought were the most peaceful and quiet places there could be. That was only in the daylight though. He saw things differently when he had to walk through a graveyard in Slough to repair the coffee machine used by the gravediggers. He didn't walk. He ran as fast as he could.

His admiration for churches was in sharp contrast to what he thought about the things that went on inside them. He detested religion of all types. Not just the ones that were often referred to as fanatics, or extremists. To him, all religion was extreme. Most people would understand why he despised the brutal regimes that imposed irrational rules on their citizens in the name of their religion and carried out barbaric punishments on anyone breaking those rules. But they might not be so understanding of his contempt for the harmless old bat in a big hat, such as his mum, who went to church every Sunday, and invariably said 'Ooh lovely service vicar' on the way out and went for a cup of tea and biscuits with her friends in the church hall afterwards. He thought the world would be a much better place without any of it. Therefore, he tried to avoid contact with the sort of people he was about to encounter.

One member of the group approached Barney, on the outdated assumption that as the man, he was the head of the family, and thrust a leaflet into his hand.

'Good afternoon. Do you mind if I ask you a few questions?'

'Yes. I do mind.'

'That's great. Do you go to church?'

'Not very often. I went once years ago, but a man in a strange costume splashed water on my head and I decided never to go again.'

The man seemed oblivious to Barney's answers.

'Do you want to know about Jesus?'

'I already know all about Jesus.'

'That's wonderful. Would you like to share what you know with me?'

'He plays for Manchester City.'

The man wasn't at all put off by the unexpected comment and continued with his efforts.

'I'm talking about Jesus who saved you. The son of our Lord.'

'How did he save me?'

'He saved all sinners.'

'Oh right, so you're saying I'm a sinner. Isn't that a little presumptuous? You've never even met me before, yet you're calling me a sinner. How dare you?'

'We're all sinners.'

'You think there are no good people in the world at all?'

'No. Apart from those who repent to the Lord.'

'Ah, I see what you mean. If a person has done nothing wrong all their life, never hurt a fly, worked at foodbanks in their spare time, and ran ten marathons in two weeks to raise money for cancer charities, they are a sinner, whereas a murderer, rapist, drug dealer, or worst of all a lying, cheating politician, just has to say 'Sorry God, I wish I hadn't done that, and I won't ever do it again, maybe", and they are first on the bus to heaven. It's all perfectly clear now. Hallelujah.'

The man was nothing if not persistent.

'Just take a look around you. God created all of these wonderful creatures for us.'

'He must have got out of the wrong side of the bed the day he created our cat.'

'Our Lord does not get out of bed.'

'Maybe it's time he did. There is a lot of suffering going on in the world. He could get to work ending some of it. Or all of it.'

He gave it one last attempt.

'Would you like to know more about Jesus?'

'No thanks. I've already told you I know everything about him.'

'I'm delighted to hear it. What would you like to tell me what you feel about him?'

'Yes, no problem. I would like to tell you that Jesus is a make-believe character from a book of fairy stories. Anyone who thinks he is real is a crank.'

'Your life would be fulfilled if you could find Jesus.'

'I didn't know he was lost.'

'I fear you are the one who is lost.'

A rainbow appeared in the sky, which momentarily spooked Barney. The man picked up on that.

'It's a sign.'

Barney recovered his composure,

'It's not a sign. It's a meteorological phenomenon that is

caused by reflection, refraction and dispersion of light in water droplets.'

'It's a sign from God.'

'I think my version is more plausible.'

'It was a sign God sent to Noah that he would never flood the world again.'

'He was a hell of a bloke that Noah. He and his wife, plus his three sons and their wives managed to build a boat which must have been the size of a cross channel ferry. Then the eight of them rounded up two of every animal in the world. They went to the north pole and grabbed a pair of polar bears, before going all the way to the south pole to pick up a penguin or two. Then they popped over to Australia to get some kangaroos, dingoes, wallabies and various other strange creatures, calling in at Africa on the way back to collect a couple of surprisingly cooperative lions, not to mention elephants, rhinoceroses and hippopotamuses. They came to England for the less exotic creatures such as squirrels and rabbits, and obviously the slugs and wasps came from England too. Not to mention a quick trip to Scotland, although it couldn't have been that quick in those days, where they managed to grab a couple of midges in order to annoy English tourists for centuries, but left the loch ness monster behind, presumably because they couldn't it's other half, then finally, they somehow crossed the Atlantic Ocean to America, which hadn't been discovered yet to pick up some bison and bald eagles. And the most extraordinary thing of all is that they did all that without falling out. Normal families couldn't have gone through all that without being at each other's throats. No wonder God wanted to save them.'

The man didn't have any rational response and just continued waffling. By this time Barney was no longer enjoying himself and was beginning to get angry.

'Listen mate. I know all about Christianity. My mum tried to drum it into me when I was a kid. You see that cross dangling from your neck? It was an instrument of torture and execution, which makes it an ideal symbol for a religion, given all the blood spilt over the centuries. Now I must leave and return to the real world. I'm not interested in your barmy beliefs. But don't worry. Some gullible fool will be along soon, and you might have better luck with them.'

The man was at last becoming disheartened and realised he was wasting his time, so he gave up and walked away. Alison stormed off in the other direction. He followed for a while, deliberately lagging behind, fearing an imminent backlash. Then she turned around and gave him both barrels.

'That was completely uncalled for. Was it necessary to be so rude? That man didn't deserve to be spoken to like that.'

'He did deserve it. He insulted my intelligence.'

'No he didn't. He was perfectly polite to you.'

'I know he was. He politely insulted my intelligence.'

'In what way did he insult your intelligence? If you had any worth insulting.'

'Put it this way. If a complete stranger came up to you uninvited and told you there were fairies and pixies living at the bottom of his garden who came out and did a dance and sang songs at midnight every night and then rode around on a unicorn, would you say "Ooh that's interesting, tell me all about it", or would you think he was a nutcase and hope he would go away?'

'That's different.'

'Not to me it isn't. It's exactly the same.'

'How can it be the same? There are millions of people all around the world that believe in a god.'

'I know. There are millions of Christians. Millions of Muslims. Millions of Jews, Hindus, Buddhists and many others. Only one of them can be right. Therefore, it means millions are wrong. Which means your reasoning is not logical. Just because millions of people think something, it doesn't mean there has to be any truth in it. They can't all be right. Most of them must be wrong. My opinion is they are all wrong. It's hardly a controversial view when you think about it.'

'You're setting a bad example to Jack.'

'On the contrary, I'm setting him a good example. It's important to teach him not to believe any old cobblers some cuckoo tells him.'

'You'd be better off telling him to keep a more open mind.'

'Thinking there could be some truth in these absurd fantasies is your idea of a more open mind?'

'Well…. I err…. You're impossible sometimes.'

'And you're a hypocrite.'

'How am I?'

'That man back there was preaching Christianity. Therefore, he was effectively telling the Hindus and Jews and all the others that their beliefs are wrong. You should be having a go at him. He was doing the same thing I was. Only he is worse. He is trying to force his opinions on innocent passers-by. I only gave my opinion when I was provoked into doing so.'

'You could have just walked on and politely told him you didn't have time to talk.'

'Too many people do just that. I'm surprised at you though. Most religions consider women to be inferior to men. I would have thought given your history you could channel your anger in that direction.'

'Okay. You might have a point on that one. But at the same time, I don't think you have any respect at all for other people's opinions.'

'Not if their opinions are loopy.'

'Some people take a great deal of comfort from their religion.'

'There must be something wrong in their lives if they have to get comfort by saying prayers to a fictional supernatural entity.'

'Sometimes you are not a very nice person.'

'I assumed you married me for the person I was, not someone you wanted to turn me into.'

'Sometimes I wish I'd never married you at all.'

'That's just charming.'

They walked on in silence and never spoke another word until they arrived at the house. By the time they got home, they were all very tired and expecting to sleep well tonight. That was the plan at least. Alison was feeling a little remorseful too, which was unusual for her. She had said something she genuinely wished she hadn't. Inside the front door she grabbed hold of his hand.

'I'm sorry about that last comment. I didn't mean the bit about wishing I'd never married you.'

'Yes you did. And I don't blame you.'

They both laughed then hugged and kissed. Barney sensed an opportunity.

'Why don't we go up to the bedroom and discuss it in more detail?'

'Don't push your luck, buster. I'm still mad at you. And I meant all those other things I said.'

Much to their relief, Jack fell asleep quickly. They went to bed, but just to sleep. For a change Barney was the first to fall asleep, which was not how things normally panned out, but he was exhausted, and it was probably for the best that he had had his amorous advances rejected. Alison was relaxed and cosy. But just as she drifted off into the darkness, she was awoken by the most horrendous ear-piercing shriek. She switched on the bedside lamp just in time to watch Mildred scurrying out of the door.

'What the hell's going on? What was that scream?'

'That little bastard has just attacked me!'

'Leave her alone. She's just a little cat.'

'A little cat with fucking sharp claws. Look. I'm bleeding.'

'Where are you bleeding?'

'In the last place a man would want to be scratched by a cat.'

Alison looked down, saw Barney desperately fumbling around for some tissues and couldn't help laughing.

'Ha, ha! She got your willy.'

'It's not funny. Look at the all the blood.'

'It serves you right for threatening to feed her rat poison.'

'That's exactly what I'm going to do. As soon as you've gone away.'

'Don't you dare.'

'Do you want her buried in the garden, or would you prefer a cremation?'

'You're the one who should be poisoned. If I'd known what it was going to be like being married to you, I would have put rat poison in your food.'

'If I'd known what it was going to be like being married to you, I would have gladly eaten it.'

This caused them both to laugh, although it was difficult for Barney with the pain. She thought she ought to be more sympathetic.

'Do you need some help with that thing?'

'No. Keep your hands off it. You had your chance earlier.'

'I wasn't suggesting anything erotic. I was just going to help you stop the bleeding.'

'No thanks. I'll manage.'

'Do you think It could also be revenge from God for your earlier blasphemy.'

'Don't be ridiculous. You don't believe in God any more than I do.'

She looked down at his injured member and his attempts to stem the flow of blood and burst out laughing again.

'I do now.'

Barney went to the bathroom to clean up and find some sort of antiseptic. It was half an hour before he got back to bed, and much longer before he got back to sleep. The only plus side he could find from this horrible incident was that it should put paid to his chances of having any more children.

After a long and restless night, Barney was in considerable pain. When Alison woke up, she wasn't exactly sympathetic. She found it quite amusing. Barney thought back to the cricketers laughing at their teammate who got hit in the balls. This was just the same. If the cat had scratched him on his arm or leg, Alison would have no doubt washed the wound for him and put a plaster on, asked if he was feeling better and brought him a cup of tea in bed. But for some reason, getting clawed on his dick was absolutely hilarious.

Alison left at 10.00. She was getting the train to London. Mary was bringing her a van full of the stuff she needed for work, that she would be driving around in all week. Barney had the rest of the day to himself, sort of, and his plans were very simple. Drink a few beers and watch the match. He just had to make sure Jack was amused. Jack was in a chatty mood, so Barney just talked to him. He tried to explain the importance of the Sunderland match but was struggling to get him interested. He reluctantly changed the subject.

'I heard mummy took you to the hairdressers?'

'Yes. It was fun. Do you go to the hairdressers?'

'No. I go to the barbers.'

'What's a barber?'

'When I was your age, girls went to the hairdressers, while the boys went to the barbers. The barber I went to was useless. He never cut hair straight. And he had a wooden leg. He used to limp around me when he was cutting my hair, and he used to sing songs and tell jokes. You shouldn't laugh at someone's disability, but for a little kid it was funny at the time.'

'Can I go to the barbers?'

'When you're older you can. For now, mummy likes to take you to the hairdressers.'

With half an hour to go before kick-off, Barney settled down on the sofa with a beer, while Jack played quietly with his toy cars. But the lack of sleep caused by his painful willy had caught up with him and he nodded off for ten minutes. When he woke up, the match was about to start, so he had a quick check on Jack. He couldn't be bothered to move, so he just shouted.

'Jack, are you alright?'

'Yes daddy. I'm just playing.'

'Oh good. Are you still playing with your cars?'

'No. I'm playing barbers.'

'That's nice.'

Five minutes later, Barney jumped up from the sofa. A terrible thought had just come into his head.

'Oh my god!'

He rushed to Jack to make sure he still had the blonde curls Alison loved some much. He did. Mostly in his hands, and the rest lying on the floor. Very little left on his head. Barney instantly knew his life was not going to be worth living when Alison found out. He considered leaving the country for a few years. But what he needed was to keep a cool head. It was going to be at least a week before Alison saw Jack. Is that long enough for hair to grow? He thought it was unlikely, but it might give him time to dream up a good excuse.

Unfortunately for him, his one-week leeway was about to disappear. His phone gave out yet another blast of Action by Def Leppard and Alison's name flashed up.

'Hello. Did you have a good journey?'

'Yes. Not too bad. It's very nice in first class.'

Barney was silently fuming but thought under the circumstances it would be better if he kept quiet.

'The hotel is very nice. We're about to go for our spa treatment. I thought I would have a chat with Jack first. Would you put him on?'

Barney made a desperate attempt to change the subject.

'How can Mary afford a spa treatment at the Dorchester?'

'She can't. I said I would treat her. We've got plenty of money.'

'We won't have for much longer the way you're spending it.'

'Don't be such a skinflint. Just put Jack on.'

Barney covered the phone with his hand and told Jack not to mention the selfie haircut. Then he handed the phone to him.

'Mummy, mummy.'

'Hello my darling. What have you been up to?'

'I've been playing with my cars. And then I was playing barbers. Do you know what a barber is?'

'Yes. I do. What exactly have you done? I hope you've not been doing something to your hair.'

'Daddy said I shouldn't mention it.'

'Did he now? Put him back on the phone.'

Barney reluctantly took the phone back from Jack, knowing that he was in for a hard time. He had to think quickly.

'What the hell have you done? Is it not safe to leave him with you for five minutes?'

'Sorry, I didn't catch that. It's a bad signal. You're breaking up.'

'When I get hold of you, I'm going to do a lot worse than what Mildred did to you.'

'No, it's no good. I can't hear. I'm losing you.'

Then he hung up. He turned to Jack and said, 'Cheers mate.'

Jack looked back at him with a grin on his face.

'Daddy. Is mummy cross with me?'

'No. She's not cross with you.'

'Is she cross with you?

'Yes, she fuc… yes, she is.'

'You nearly said a naughty word. I'll tell mummy.'

'Jesus Christ.'

'You told that man Jesus wasn't real.'

13

Barney had managed to get Jack to go to bed without any trouble, which was a big bonus. For tonight at least he would forget about Jack's hair and worry about facing Alison later. He could now have a relaxing evening in front of the television, watching all the things he liked for a change. But his relaxing didn't last long. He was disturbed by another burst of Action by Def Leppard. It was Liam. He was driving his car and was on the hands free.

'Hi mate. I need your help. I'm travelling tonight for my training course which is happening in the morning. But I'm having a bit of trouble getting there.'

'I can give it a go. Where are you trying to get to?'

'Turkey.'

'Turkey! Are you sure about that?'

'Yes. But when I put it in my satnav, it says it's 2537 miles and will take 39 hours.'

'It can't be Turkey. Someone must be having a laugh at your expense.'

They wouldn't be the first ones, would they?'

'Don't be so touchy. What training are you doing?'

'The Cafeblam 73. The same one you and Colin went on.'

Barney held his head in his hands.

'That was Torquay.'

'That's what I said. Anyhow, I phoned Colin and he told me to take the M4 to just past Bristol, then join the M5 and take it all the way to junction 31. But I'm on the M5 now and the junction numbers are going lower. I joined on Junction 15, and I've just gone past junctions 14 and 13.'

'You've gone in the wrong direction. You have taken the northbound M5 instead of the southbound.'

'What shall I do?'

'When you get to junction 12, take the slip road, go around the roundabout and re-join the motorway.'

Barney ended the call. He couldn't believe what he was hearing. He knew Liam had been feeling stressed lately, but even by his standards this was ridiculous. There was worse to come. His phone played Action by Def Leppard again.

'I did what you said. But the next junction I passed was junction 11.'

Barney was close to banging his head against the wall.

'Didn't you get off at junction 12 and go around the roundabout?'

'Yes. That's exactly what I did.'

'When I said go around the roundabout, I didn't mean all the way around. I meant go halfway and join the motorway in the other direction. Try that when you get to junction 10. Then try putting Torquay into your satnav.'

'I've already tried to. But it comes up as an invalid destination.'

'How are you spelling it?'

'T O R K E Y.'

'It's T O R Q U A Y.'

Liam tried it.

'Yes, that seems to have worked. It's only 130 miles away. Thanks.'

'Have a nice time. I can recommend a cracking pub just a short walk along the sea front. You may need to escape at some point. I certainly did. Do you know the name of the bloke taking the course?'

'I was told to ask for Phil.'

'That's who I had. You're in for a treat. He talks in euphemisms, daft slogans, and his own version of cockney rhyming slang. Most of the things he comes out with are just gibberish, and half the time I couldn't understand what the hell he was talking about. And he's supposed to be teaching you. And his assistant had a huge yellow spot on the end of his nose which was very distracting, but I would hope that would be gone by now.'

'I look forward to it. I was supposed to meet him this evening at an introductory meeting, but I'm going to be really late getting there now.'

'Not as late as you have been if you'd have tried to drive to Turkey. Or if you'd have stayed on the northbound M6. You could have popped in and said hello to my mum.'

It was 9.30 by the time Liam had made it to the hotel. The official welcoming meeting was over, but Phil, his assistant, and a few of the other trainees were still in the bar. Liam had phoned the number he had been given, and Phil came out to meet him.

'Glad you could make it. Did you have a good Eric and Ernie?'

'Erm…'

'Go to the bar and meet the others. I'll be back in a few minutes. I've just got to take the Browns to the super bowl.'

Liam replied, 'I see', but didn't really see. Then when he eventually worked out what Phil must have meant, he just wanted to say 'yuk!'

Liam could see that Barney hadn't been exaggerating. And although he was a lot more tolerant than Barney, it wasn't going to take long to get hacked off listening to this sort of stuff. He bought a pint and introduced himself to the others. He instantly understood why Barney went out to find a decent pub when he was here. But Liam wasn't as comfortable going to a pub on his own. Instead, he decided to wander out to find somewhere to get a pizza, which fortunately wasn't very far away, and he took it back to his room where he watched television until he fell asleep.

The early night had paid dividends the next morning. When Barney was here, he had to cope with a hangover, as well as people he didn't like, whereas Liam's biggest difficulty was understanding the training. As well as the drivel spouted by Phil, he couldn't take on board the technical complexities of the Cafeblam 73.

After a difficult morning, Phil declared there would be an hour for lunch.

'Feel free to go and spill some produce down the rabbit hole, and we'll meet back here at two chirps of the cuckoo.'

Liam wasn't usually one for turning away food, but he didn't go to the restaurant. Instead, he went to his room and returned a phone call which he had missed an hour earlier. It was the call he had been eagerly waiting to hear. He now had no intention of seeing out the rest of the day. He had the good manners to go to Phil and lie his way out of it.

'My wife has just gone into labour. I've got to rush back immediately.'

'Congratulations. I didn't realise your wife had bacon in the drawer. You'd better go. Do you want to take the service manual for the Cafeblam 73 and some useful part numbers and technical helpline phone numbers?'

'No thanks. I won't be needing them.'

'In that case I'll bid you adios. I hope it all goes well with the dustbin.'

Liam just said goodbye. He'd long ago given up trying to figure out what Phil was talking about. As soon as he was on the way home, he called Mary.

'Hi. I have some news for you.'

Following that call he phoned Barney and told him the same news. Then he told him about his training course.

'I see what you mean about Phil. He was coming out with some strange sentences. Even when I was leaving, the last thing he said to me was something about good luck with the dustbin.'

'That could have been dustbin lid. Cockney rhyming slang for kid.'

'But he's not even a cockney. He's got an ooh arrrr sort of accent. But that would explain it. I pretended I was rushing back because my wife was in labour. But he was coming out with some drivel.'

'I know. At least you had an excuse to leave halfway through. I had to put up with it for the whole day, with a hangover, sitting next to someone who wouldn't stop sniffing.'

'Yeah, there was one of those too. You'd think grown-ups could learn how to blow their nose. Anyway, how's the injury?'

'What injury?'

'I heard you were attacked by the cat.'

'I don't believe this. Can nothing ever be kept a secret around here?'

'Where did it scratch you?'

'In the b edroom.'

'No, I mean whereabout on you?'

'You know fine well.'

'So, it's true. It was your Aladdin's lamp.'

'Why do you call it that?'

'Because when you get a girl to rub it, something magical happens.'

'I'll tell you what. If mine could grant me three wishes, the first one would be to turn that cat into a rabbit. And then I'd make a casserole out of it. For the second one I would wish that my wife wouldn't tell personal things to the biggest blabbermouth in the company. And before you say it, yes that's your fucking girlfriend I'm talking about.'

14

Mary was enjoying her Sauna. Alison wasn't.

'I'm going to kill him. I am really going to kill him.'

'Relax. It's not the end of the world. It's quite funny when you think about it.'

Alison didn't see the funny side at all. The comment by Mary just made her even more angry. If she wasn't in a sauna, you could probably see steam coming out of her ears.

'Do you think so? I don't find it remotely funny. How would you feel if you couldn't trust Liam to look after Louis?'

'Are you for real? I wouldn't trust Liam to look after a pint of lager. Let's face it, all men are useless. Forget about it. Let's go to the bar and have a few drinks, then we can get ready to go out. Forget all about Jack and his hair, and your intention to murder your husband. You can do that any time. Let's just go and enjoy ourselves.'

Mary's wise words had the desired effect. The aftermath of the sauna, steam room, and jacuzzi, plus a few Bacardi and cokes had chilled Alison out to the extent where she had temporarily forgotten all about Jack's hair and was starting to enjoy herself. Later, they ended up in an upmarket nightclub in the West End, a place with prices that would have horrified Barney. But they didn't care. They were having fun. Mary kept pointing out all the single men and made crude suggestions about what she would like to do to them. Alison found it funny and knew Mary would run a mile if one of them came up to her. And it did happen. Two young men approached them and one of them said, 'Can I buy you ladies a drink?'

Alison was very abrupt with them.

'No thanks', she answered, then turned away. The young men trudged away, rejected. Mary wasn't happy.

'What did you say that for? They were only going to buy us a drink.'

'We don't need them to buy us a drink. I've got way more money than they have.'

'It's not about the money. Aren't you flattered those two handsome young men are interested in us?'

'I'm the opposite of flattered. They just see us as easy targets. What do you think they are going to want in return for the drink?'

'So what? You're not going to get any of that at home for a while after what the cat did to Barney.'

'You're not seriously suggesting that I …'

'Why not?'

'Don't be ridiculous. If you think I'm going to …'

'I know, I know. Calm down. I'm only joking. But a free drink and a dance wouldn't have harmed anyone.'

'Forget the free drink. I agree a dance would be good. Let's hit the floor.'

They spent another two hours alternating between dancing and drinking and having a really good laugh. They even had a dance with the two young men Alison had sent packing earlier.

Mary wanted to catch her last train home from Waterloo

station. That suited Alison, who was starting to feel a little strange, and wanted to get back to the hotel. So they headed for the nearest underground station, Leicester Square. They took separate tube trains. Mary took the Northern line to Waterloo, while Alison took the Piccadilly line to Hyde Park Corner.

Once Alison was on her own, she realised she wasn't feeling too well at all. She'd obviously had a lot to drink, but this was different to how she usually felt when she was drunk. She was feeling dizzy and confused. She was vaguely aware that it was only three stops to Hyde Park Corner. But something was very wrong. She was now becoming frightened and was desperately trying not to panic. The train arrived at her stop, but when she got to her feet to leave the train, her legs didn't respond properly. She couldn't remember where she was, or where she'd been. Or where she was going. A man caught hold of her and propped her up.

'You look like you're struggling, darling. Allow me to help you.'

By now Alison was completely helpless. She wasn't able to do anything to stop the man helping her out of the station and bundling her into the back of a car.

15

Barney had to take Jack to his mum's house on Monday morning where he would be staying for the week, then he would be heading back down to Winchester. He hadn't heard from Alison this morning. He supposed she was still angry about Jack's haircutting exploits. He would call her later when she'd be finished working. Hopefully she would have calmed down by then.

The journey from his house to his mum's bed and breakfast, where he has stayed many times during his working days because it was a free holiday, was less than thirty miles, but was slow. The road was narrow and wound its way up and down hills. Although the scenery was incredibly beautiful, he couldn't completely enjoy it. He was bombarded by silly questions from Jack and felt guilty he didn't have more patience with him. His intolerance of annoying adults he frequently encountered had not been the ideal preparation to be a parent. He also had to focus on the other road users. Many of them drove too fast and without any consideration for other drivers. He was about to encounter one of those.

They were just approaching a particularly high and twisty bit of road. Jack looked at some sheep scattered around the hillside and asked, 'Daddy. Are there any elephants here?'

'No. You don't get many elephants around these parts.'

'Why not?'

Before he could think of an answer, he was distracted by a sporty looking car close behind him.

'What the hell is this arsehole trying to do? There's no way of overtaking here.'

'What's an arsehole, daddy?'

'The man driving the car behind us is one. But it's not a nice word, so you shouldn't say it.'

'But you just said it.'

'I know. I shouldn't have. I'm sorry.'

'I'll tell mummy.'

'I'm sure you will, you little snitch.'

'What's a snitch?'

'It's what you are. Do you know that time when I squirted the cat with the hosepipe? I told you not to tell mummy. But you did. That's what a snitch does.'

The car was still close behind him. He could read the number plate, which was L4 RRY. Personalised number plates were one of the things he couldn't stand. He thought anyone who needed one of those must be a shallow prat with an enormous ego. The only personalised number plate that was needed was AR5 0LE, as it would describe perfectly anyone who had one. This particular driver was proving the point.

Jack wasn't interested in the car behind. He just wanted to know why there were no elephants. Barney tried to answer him.

'They are mainly in Africa, or India, so you don't... Jesus Christ, what the hell is this moron trying to do?'

The car was suddenly inches behind him and was weaving around, looking as if the driver was desperately trying to get past. Barney would have happily let him go, but there weren't any easy overtaking places. A few minutes later, Barney was getting pissed off with the situation and stubbornly slowed down. There was no way he was going to be bullied off the road. He took the stance that if he wants me to go faster, I'm going to go slower. This went on for two more miles. The driver in the car behind was blaring his horn and making gestures with his hand. Barney's response was to slow down even more.

The inevitable happened. Barney had to take a very tight turn and slowed down to almost a stop. The car behind smashed into the back of his. For the next few minutes nothing happened. He just sat in silence for a while. He wasn't keen on getting out of the car. The other driver was probably a right hard nut, and they were out here in the middle of nowhere, where nobody could see them. But looking in his mirror, he couldn't see any movement from him. He took a while to calm himself down, and to check Jack was alright. Jack looked a bit shocked, but fortunately unhurt. Eventually he summoned the courage to get out of the car and slowly walked to the other car. The man, assumably called Larry was slumped over the steering wheel and appeared to be unconscious, or even dead. Barney guessed that he must had hit his head during the crash. He phoned an ambulance.

The first vehicle on the scene wasn't an ambulance. It was a police car. Two police officers got out of the car and surveyed the scene. Much to his astonishment he recognised one of them. He had met this cop a few years back under unusual circumstances. He approached Barney but didn't appear to remember him.

'Good morning. I'm Sergeant Price. Are you the driver of this car?'

Barney made a point of taking a long, slow look around the deserted landscape before answering.

'No. It wasn't me. Honest, officer.'

'Are you trying to be funny?'

'Yes. Are you?'

'Would you prefer to continue this conversation down at the police station?'

'I think you've been watching too many episodes of Midsomer Murders. Of course I'm the driver. The only other conscious person anywhere near here is my four-year-old son. And he doesn't do much driving. And if it helps with your enquiries, the driver of the other car is the bloke slumped over his steering wheel.'

Their conversation was interrupted by the arrival of an ambulance. The two policemen and Barney stood in silence watching as the man was helped out of the car, put on a stretcher, and taken into the ambulance.

After the ambulance disappeared into the distance with sirens blazing and blue lights flashing, Sergeant Price turned his attention back to Barney.

'We would like you to come down the station to answer a few questions.'

'And if I choose not to?'

'Then I'll arrest you.'

'What would be the charge?'

'Dangerous driving for starters. Could be a lot worse, depending on the condition of the other driver.'

'Are you for real? I dangerously let someone drive their car into the back of mine?'

But Barney knew he had little choice, given the possibly serious condition of the other driver. He had to go to the police station.

When he was walking back to the car, he overheard Sergeant Price talking to his colleague.

'I'm sure I've seen him somewhere before. I can't remember where, but I'm sure he's a wrong'n. When we get back to the station, find out who he is and see if he's got a record.'

When they arrived at the police station, they had provided someone to look after Jack while Barney was taken to an interview room.

The interview started with Price asking, 'Would you mind telling me what happened?'

'Not at all. The car followed me for a few miles. He was far too close. He was obviously desperate to get past. Then he crashed into me. There was nothing I could do.'

'That's for us to decide.'

'There's nothing to decide. He drove into the back of me. End of story. He is an idiot.'

'That's no way to talk about a dead man.'

'How do you know he's dead? He's probably only arriving at the hospital now.'

'He looked dead.'

'Oh I see, so the new official policy of the police in these circumstances is, assumed dead until proved not quite so dead? Hadn't you better wait until you actually have confirmation.'

'Don't worry. We'll confirm it. And you were right there when it happened. So you're in the frame.'

'Right. Another new policy. If someone is found dead, the murderer must have been the first person you can find who was anywhere near the victim at the time. Let's face it Sergeant Prick, you haven't a clue what you're doing.'

'My name is Price, not Prick.'

'I'm sure it is.'

'I've met you somewhere before, haven't I?'

'Yes, you have'.

'I knew it. And I'm sure when I check up on you, I'll find you have a string of criminal convictions.'

'No. I don't have any criminal convictions at all. Although assaulting a police officer is very tempting right now.'

'We can add threatening a police officer to your charges.'

'Oh do leave off. You know me because you're a friend of my mum. Elizabeth Barnard. About five years ago she phoned you to report me missing, even though I was only in the pub where I told her I was going. You turned up and ruined my evening.'

Price paused a while to take it all in. This revelation appeared to change his tone completely.

'Don't think you're going to get any special treatment just because I'm friends with your mum.'

'I don't want any special treatment. I don't need it. The other driver, either dead or alive was clearly to blame. You don't have a case, Sergeant Prick. Can I go now?'

'Ok. I wouldn't want to upset Elizabeth. We'll take no further action.'

'That's your idea of getting no special treatment. Is there more to your friendship that you're not telling me about?'

'Be careful what you're saying. I could change my mind and charge you with manslaughter or something. Your mum is a very dear friend of mine. I sometimes do favours for her.'

'I'd rather not know about the favours. And because you are friends with my mum, I'm going to give you special treatment and not tell you what I think of your policing skills. Goodbye.'

On the way out, the other policeman who was at the scene came in and told them that the other driver was alive and well. It turns out he'd had a mild heart attack while driving and had been desperate to get past Barney's car to get to the hospital. Barney collected Jack and continued his interrupted journey.

He wasn't sure how much he should tell his mum about what just happened. He didn't know exactly how much of a friend she was with the cop, but Price soon changed his attitude quite dramatically when he found he was her son. In the end he opted to tell her nothing. If Price said anything to her, he would deal with it later.

Soon after arrival at his mum's house he checked his phone. Alison hadn't called. But the name Sweary was showing five missed calls. He called her back straight away, and she answered immediately.

'Where the fuck have you been? I've been trying to call you all day.'

'Sorry. I've been helping the police with their enquiries. What's up?'

'I was wondering what happened to Alison. She didn't arrive for work this morning. I've been trying to call her, but I'm getting no answer.'

'That's strange. I'll try calling her. I'll let you know when I hear anything,'

He was very concerned now. He could understand if her phone had stopped working, but he couldn't think of a reason why she wouldn't have turned up at the Vendetta office. He rang Alison's number twice, but got no answer. All he could think of doing next was to ring the Dorchester Hotel. They told him they would look into it and call him back. After fifteen minutes, which seemed like hours, they called him back. What they told him was extremely disturbing. She hadn't checked in for breakfast and hadn't checked out of the hotel this morning. Her company van was still in the car park, and her room key hadn't been used since yesterday afternoon. In other words, she hadn't returned to the hotel after her night out.

16

Alison slowly regained consciousness and tried to figure out what had happened to her. Her mind was still confused. The last thing she remembered was getting on the tube, but nothing else after that. She was in a small room with light coming through a tiny window, lying on a bed. There was a hard wooden chair in the room. It looked very similar to the sort of room you get in a quaint little guest house in the countryside. She tried to stand up, but couldn't. Her ankles were tied together, and her hands were tied behind her back. She was tempted to scream and shout, in the hope that someone would hear her and come to the rescue. But she opted not to. She decided to wait until her head was clear, and the best course of action would be to wait until she found out exactly why she was here, and who was behind this.

She presumed she had been drugged, possibly with one of those date rape drugs she had heard mentioned quite often in the newspapers, and on television. She tried to think when it could have happened. She had refused drinks from the two young men in the club, therefore someone must have put something in a drink she had left on the table when she went dancing, or when she went to the toilet. She wondered about Mary. Was her drink spiked too? If so, where is she now. Has someone captured her too?

She lay there for what seemed like an hour, with all kinds of questions running through her head. Who was behind this? Why have they done it? How have they done it? What is going to happen next? But she wasn't ready for the shock she was about to receive. A door opened, and suddenly everything became much clearer, but more confusing at the same time. Through the door walked Kenneth.

'Hello Alison. I hope you are comfortable.'

'What the hell? What's going on? Why have you done this? Untie me now! Now!'

'Calm down my dear. Let's be civilised about this.'

'Civilised? You drug me, kidnap me, and tie me up. Then you tell me to act civilised. You piece of shit. Untie me and let me go.'

'You will be free to go soon enough. But before that can be allowed, some things are going to have to happen first.'

'What sort of things?'

'It has come to my attention that your husband is incredibly wealthy. It would be good if he could generously donate some of his money to a worthy cause. Or more specifically, to me.'

'You've got no chance. He is strongly against giving in to blackmailers or kidnappers.'

'Let's ask him then, shall we?'

'You're wasting your time. He won't give you a penny.'

'That would be most unfortunate for you. Because if he doesn't play ball, you won't be getting out of here alive.'

The threat didn't worry Alison.

'Don't you dare threaten me. You won't get away with this.'

'I think I will. But if he doesn't come up with the money, there is another way out of this for you.'

'And what would that be?'

'Come back to me.'

'Never in a million years. I would rather die. The day I got divorced from you was the happiest day of my life.'

17

Barney had tried calling Alison again at regular intervals throughout the day, but to no avail. He checked again with Mary to see if she had turned up at the Vendetta office, or had been in touch. On Tuesday morning he had reached the point where he realised he was getting nowhere and thought he ought to report her missing. He went back to the same police station he was needlessly taken to only yesterday. He reported to the reception desk and gave a brief summary of why he was there. He was told to take a seat and someone would be with him shortly. Much to his dismay, the someone was Sergeant Price.

'Well, well, well. What have we here? Imagine seeing you again in here so soon.'

'Cut the Dixon of Dock Green crap and listen. This is serious.'

'I'm all ears.'

'My wife has gone missing.'

'I see. When your mum reported to us that you were missing, you had a right go at her and said she was being ridiculous, yet here you are doing the same thing.'

'It's hardly the same thing. I had only walked around the corner to the pub, which she already knew I was going to. And she only had to try phoning me. And I had only been out for four hours It's not the same at all. This is serious, and I'd appreciate it if you would try to do your job properly.'

Price gave the impression of not being too interested in

whatever Barney was going to tell him. He took out a notebook and pen.

'Right. What is the name of this alleged missing person?'

'A notebook? Is this Z Cars? Have you not heard of computers?

'Just answer the question.'

'Alison Barnard.'

'And where is she missing.'

'How the hell should I know? That's the thing when someone is missing. You don't know where they are. Have you ever done this sort of stuff before?'

'Look. If you want my help on this, I think you need to be a little less aggressive and start answering my questions. When did you last see her?'

Barney paused and took a deep breath. He needed to calm down. It wouldn't help matters if he got stroppy.

'Sunday morning. Then I spoke to her on the phone on Sunday afternoon.'

'Where was her last known location?'

'The Dorchester Hotel in London.'

'It's alright for some.'

'No, Sergeant Prick. It's not alright for her. She is missing.'

Price asked a few more questions and made notes.

'That's all we can do at the moment. Let me know if you get any new information, or if your wife or anyone else contacts you. And my name is Price.'

Barney left the station thinking it had all been a complete waste of time. He had no confidence that Sergeant Price had any ability to do anything to help find Alison. He didn't have any idea what he could do next. There wasn't anything. All he could do was wait patiently and hope she would eventually get in touch.

18

Alison looked with loathing at her ex-husband. He looked back at her with a creepy, smug look on his face.

'Where are we?'

'We're in a holiday cottage I rented. It's in the lake district, about fifteen miles from your house. I thought it would be easier to conduct negotiations with your husband from here.'

'How did you get me here? Was I unconscious all the way from London?'

'Yes. You were under the influence of some strong drugs. You ought to be more careful what you drink.'

'Very funny. I still can't figure out how you managed to pull it off. And how do you know where we live?'

'It took a lot of hard work and planning. But I couldn't have done it without the help of one of your gullible colleagues at Vendetta.'

'What do you mean?'

'Let's just say, one of your not too bright friends gave me the opportunity to come up with this scheme.'

'Let me guess. Liam?'

'Correct. He's not the sharpest tool in the box. In fact, he's more like the metric adjustable spanner in the box.'

'What are you talking about?'

'Ask you smartarse husband to explain it. That's if you ever see him again. Liam was the only one who was friendly to me during my one day at Vendetta. He was eager to talk to me. He told me you were millionaires. He also gave me your address when I pretended that I wanted to send you a Christmas card. And he most helpfully told me his girlfriend and you were having a night out in London. The rest was easy. Perhaps not exactly easy, but I'm a lot smarter than you give me credit for.'

'How did you give me the drugs?'

'That was the easiest bit of all. I'm a bit of an expert. I've spiked women's drinks with date rape drugs several times before.'

'You are sick.'

'Soon to be sick and rich. Which reminds me, it's time to start the ball rolling. I'll be making my terms clear this afternoon.'

'How am I supposed to eat, and sleep, and go to the toilet?'

'There's a bathroom attached to this room. I will partly untie you. You can use the bed to sleep. But I must warn you against trying to escape. I've got a cricket bat over there. I can just as easily hand you back with two broken legs. I will bring you things to eat. After all, I know all your favourite food.'

'No you don't. We only ever ate all the things you wanted. Everything we did was what you wanted. You were a cowardly, controlling bully.'

'Now don't be so bitter. I remember your favourite cigarettes. I've bought you some. You must be desperate for one.'

'No actually. I'm not. I haven't smoked for years. Don't you get it yet? I decided it was time to get rid of the shit in my life that was causing me harm. Then soon after that I gave up smoking too.'

'That's a bit nasty. You'd better be careful how you talk to me. I can only tolerate so much, and then you will start to suffer.'

Alison shuddered. She knew Kenneth could be nasty, but this was an entirely different level of evil.

'Now I must leave you for a while. Just you take it easy. I'm off to start the negotiations. See you later.'

Kenneth left the room, leaving Alison thinking things over. She wondered if he meant what he said about the cricket bat. He had never been physically violent towards her. But then again, he had never abducted anyone before. Or maybe he had. He had made a disturbingly good job of it. She never would have thought he was capable of using date rape drugs on people either.

19

Barney was at a loss what to do. He jumped out of his skin every time his phone rang. This time it was Roy who was calling.'

'Hello mate. I was just calling to let you know the details of the pub we're playing in on Thursday.'

Barney had expected to be in London again this week, and was going to take the opportunity to make another appearance for the Mickey Mouse Club darts team.

'I'm really sorry Roy. Something unexpected had cropped up. It looks like I will have to drop out.'

'That's a shame. Nothing serious I hope.'

'Yes, I'm afraid it could be. But I'd rather not go into it at the moment.'

'No problem. Let me know if anything changes, or if there's anything I can do.'

'Thanks. Give my best wishes to the team.'

'I will. Just to let you know, the Cornwall trip looks like it's going ahead next month. The arrangements are going well, and hopefully we'll see you there.'

'Hopefully. But I can't say I am definitely going at this stage. I need to sort this problem out first. I'll be in touch as soon as I know anything.'

They ended the call, and almost immediately his phone went off again. And once again he jumped out of his skin. The situation was making him nervous. But it was only his mum.

'I was just calling to let you know how Jack was. 'How's thing going down there?'

'Sorry mum, I forgot to tell you, I didn't go. Something cropped up and I'm still at home. If Jack gets a bit much for you, I'll collect him.'

'He's fine. I don't think you should have cut off his hair though. I loved those blonde curls.'

'Yes. So did Alison.'

Barney was close to tears. A horrible thought had just come into his head.

He'd forgotten about jack. He tried to hold himself together. His mum was oblivious to it. She was used to Barney being moody. She was just pleased to be looking after Jack.

'He's such a lovely boy.'

'Are you sure we're talking about the same Jack?'

He ended the call. Then the phone rang yet again. This time there was no name or number on the screen. He answered, and the call lasted less than a minute before the caller ended it. Barney was numb. He sat motionless, and in silence for a few minutes. Then he drove to the police station and asked for Sergeant Price. The Sergeant's demeanour never seemed to change, no matter what the circumstances. He wasn't remotely concerned at the distress Barney was obviously in. He liked to use old fashioned methods. He took out a notebook and pencil again. He would write everything down and worry about putting it on a computer later.

'Right. About this alleged phone call you received….'

'What do you mean alleged? There's nothing alleged about it Sergeant Pri… er Price. It was a real call. I didn't fucking imagine it.'

'No need for the language. This phone call. Was there a number on the screen?'

'Of course there fuc… No. There wasn't.'

'I thought there wouldn't be. Hostage takers are usually good at covering their tracks.'

'That's really well worked out. Are you sure you've done this kind of thing before? Don't you have specialist teams for dealing with kidnappers?'

'It may come to that. But for the moment, I'm all you've got. It's my case. Now tell me exactly what the caller said.'

'He said he had Alison. He wants me to give him a quarter of a million pounds.'

'Ha ha. That's ridiculous. It must be a hoax. Where does he expect you to get that sort of money?'

'I already have that sort of money. And obviously he knows I do.'

Price was beginning to think Barney was a bit of a fantasist.

'Right. So, what are you going to do?'

'I was hoping you might be able to tell me.'

'You could always pay him.'

'Wow! You're on fire today. If I was just going to pay him, I wouldn't be coming around here wasting my time talking to you.'

'What did they say would happen if you didn't pay?'

'That they would kill Alison.'

'Do you think they mean it.'

'How would I know. This sort of thing doesn't happen to me every day.'

'No. Right. I hope you don't mind me asking this, but does Elizabeth know about this?'

'No, not yet. But she'll have to find out sooner or later. Why is that any of your business?'

'I'm just concerned for her. I'll be seeing her on Sunday. We sit next to each other in church.'

'Wonderful. The fate of my wife is in the hands of some fruitcake who sings songs to the great sky wizard.'

'You are really trying my patience. You're lucky it's not thirty years ago. Police brutality wasn't frowned upon the way it is these days. You wouldn't have got away with talking to me like that.'

'That's not very Christian of you.'

'Don't you dare mock my faith.'

Why not? 'If this god of yours was anything like the all-powerful, all loving geezer he's cracked up to be, he wouldn't have let Alison get kidnapped in the first place.'

20

Barney generally enjoyed visiting Sunderland. The football often ruined the enjoyment, but there were plenty times when it was enhanced by a good result. He wasn't all that keen on the climate. It was usually a couple of degrees colder than Maidenhead, but that didn't stop fans going to the game in just a short-sleeved football shirt. Barney wrapped up in the biggest coat he thought he could get away with without looking like a softy southerner. One of the things he liked best was the cost of a pint, and the cost of most other things. It didn't matter so much now he was rich, but it was handy in the days of his financial woes. He liked the people. Or at least he liked most of them. He thought they were much friendlier than they were in the south, but weren't shy in giving their opinion. That was probably why he liked them. There were plenty of arguments to be had. This particular visit wasn't intended to give him pleasure. It was a visit driven by desperation.

He had a friend called Neil who lived in Sunderland. They had met in a pub when he was up there to watch a match at the Stadium of Light. Barney had been throwing darts, and Neil asked him if he wanted a game. They played a few games and got talking afterwards, and they became good friends. Ever since then they would meet up for a drink, and sometimes a game of darts whenever Barney had got the chance to make the long journey from Maidenhead to see a game. They would meet in a pub called the Cliff, which was near to where the old Roker Park used to be, but was still close enough to the new stadium to be able to drink there before a match. When he couldn't make it to games, Neil would send him messages giving his account of how the team performed.

Neil was a private investigator. Barney didn't know how good he was at his job. They never talked about work much. But Barney was desperate for any help he could get, and he knew Neil was someone he could trust. He sent him an Email, and he was soon on the way to Sunderland. It wasn't such a long drive from the lake district as it used to be when he had to travel from Maidenhead. Just over two hours after he set off, he was in the Cliff and met Neil.

'Thanks for coming at such short notice.'

'It's nee problem mate. I only live half a mile down the road. You're the one who has had to travel far. Besides, you sounded as if you were in big trouble. How can I help?'

Neil listened while Barney explained everything.

'Bloody hell! That's awful. Obviously I'll help you as much as I can. But I can't officially take the case. I'm flying to America in two days, and won't be back for a fortnight.'

'Oh. In that case you won't be much use. I suspect it will all be resolved one way or the other by the time you get back. But I would appreciate any advice. Do you have any suggestions what I can do?'

Neil was deep in thought for a while, churning the information over in his head.

'You say you kept your lottery win a secret. But the person behind this obviously knows about it. So that must narrow it down. I know rumours can easily get around, but how many people definitely know about it?'

'Alison. But she wouldn't fake her own kidnapping.'

'It wouldn't be the first time someone has done that.'

Barney paused for a while.

'No. Rule that one out. That's not remotely feasible.'

'Who else then?'

'Our close friends Liam and Mary. But you can rule them out too.'

'Are you sure?'

'Yes. Come on. You need to do better than this.'

'Okay. Does anyone else know?'

'The other members of my darts team. And they all won a share of the money too. They would have no need to do this. But they wouldn't do it anyway. They are my friends.'

'Keep thinking.'

'My mum and dad. But before you say anything, I'm ruling them out too.'

'Well it must have been somebody. Think hard.'

'The only other person who knew was my old boss Richard Bowles He was standing right next to me at a Christmas party when I received the news.'

'Now we're getting somewhere. Tell me about him. Did you get on well?'

'No. We were constantly arguing. I made his life quite difficult.'

'He sounds like a prime suspect to me.'

'No. He can't have done it. He's in hospital at the moment,

very ill. Besides, I would have recognised his voice on the phone. Come to think of it, I would have recognised the voice of any of the people we have just mentioned.'

'It doesn't mean they aren't behind it. This Bowles character could have other people involved. It could be worth mentioning to this cop.'

'I will. But he's useless. He isn't going to be any help.'

What about that gang you had trouble with? They sounded like a bad bunch. And from what you told me about it, your karate mate left one of them with a badly broken arm.'

'I flattened one of them too.'

'Wow. He must have been a tough guy.'

'Very funny.'

'Also, you didn't pay them all of the money they said you owed them. Is it possible they are looking for revenge?'

'I very much doubt it. They were just a pair of clowns playing at gangsters. The toy gun they pointed at me was pathetic. They wouldn't have the intelligence to arrange an abduction.'

'There is another person you haven't mentioned who knows about your financial situation.'

'And who might that be?'

'Me.'

'Are you the kidnapper?'

'Nar man. You're missing the point. That's why I'm the sharp minded private investigator, and you're just a vending machine repair man. I work with a very logical process.'

'Vending machines and their users aren't logical. You have to think outside the box. That's why I'm a sharp minded vending machine repair man and you are just a private investigator.'

'Ok. No need to get all defensive.'

'What is your point?'

'Do you remember when you told me you had won the lottery?'

'No.'

'Exactly.'

'Still not with you.'

'Do you remember last season, when we knocked Manchester United out of the FA Cup?'

'Like I'm going to forget that.'

'We went on the lash around Sunderland city centre. While you were inebriated, you told me about your lottery win. You still expected me to pay for my drinks though.'

'And?'

'You're always getting pissed. You could have told anyone and didn't realise.'

'Terrific. The professional advice of a sharp minded private investigator is that it could be anyone. That's enormously helpful.'

'I'm only giving you the facts. Going back to the phone call. You say you would have recognised the voice if it was someone you knew. Was there anything about the voice that sounded familiar?'

'Yes. I had a feeling I'd heard him somewhere before. I just can't remember where from. I think he was putting on an accent that wasn't really his.'

'That's a typical ploy in situations like this.'

'Where do I go from here?'

'I still think this Bowles gadgee is worth looking at.'

'Do you think I should pay up?'

'I can't answer that. I really feel for you, but there's no right or wrong answers in a case like this. I've seen it before. You could pay, and then they get greedy and ask for more. Or you could call their bluff and not pay, and then they go through with their threat and kill her.'

'I guessed as much. Thanks anyway. Enjoy America, and we'll meet up for a match soon if I get through all this.'

'Aye. I'll stay in touch while I'm out there, and I'll call you when I get back. If it's still not resolved, I'll help you in any way I can.'

They finished their drink and Barney went back to his car. He sat for a while thinking. The meeting with Neil hadn't helped as much as he wanted. He'd gone to him more in desperation than realistic expectation. He'd never been in a situation like this before. He'd spent most of his life getting angry at life's trivial irritations, and at the sort of people who made his life difficult. This situation was on a different level. He was out of his comfort zone. He thought about his wife and what she might be going through. Then he thought about Jack and tears ran down his face, He'd forgotten about Jack. How was he going to tell him he wasn't going to see his mum again? He'd never felt so helpless and alone.

He sat in his car for half an hour, then pulled himself together and realised he needed to get home. As he drove away, he couldn't imagine Bowles being behind this. But Neil could have a point. And he had nothing else. He stopped the car and called Mary.

21

'Mary. The cop who is dealing with the case wants to speak with you. I told him I would let you know, and I gave him your number.'

'Why does he want to speak to me?'

'It'll be just routine. You were the last person to see her. He's hoping you might remember some small detail which could give a clue as to what happened.'

'But there's nothing to tell. I walked to Leicester Square tube station with her, then we took separate trains.'

'I know. But we have to do anything that might help. To be honest, I have no faith in him at all. He's been a cop for years, but is probably more used to dealing with people who've had their bike stolen, or little old ladies with their cat stuck up a tree. Maybe the odd rowdy tourist who can't take their drink. But, as he just reminded me, we have to deal with him at the moment.'

'Ok. I look forward to his call. Or do I have to meet him in person?'

'I don't know. But it would be unreasonable of him to expect you to come all this way, and I doubt he's ever been south of Manchester all his life. Do you mind if I ask you a question?'

'No. Fire away.'

'How many people at Vendetta knew about my lottery win?'

'In theory, Richard Bowles, Liam and I. But you know what

it's like at work. Word always gets around. Why?'

'I'm just trying to figure something out. Is Bowles still in hospital?'

'Yes. Wait a minute. You don't seriously think he's the mastermind behind this, do you? He was drugged up and doolally when I visited him. But he did go particularly crazy when I mentioned your name.'

'Charming. I think I might pay him a visit. How would you like to come with me?'

'I wouldn't like it at all. But I'll do it if you think it might help.'

'I'm on my way.'

Barney headed south straight from Sunderland. There was no point in going home first. He could buy a change of clothes, and anything else he needed. He sometimes forgot how well off he was. He had forced himself to have a new determination. He wasn't going to help Alison or Jack by worrying about himself. It would be more productive to stop thinking about himself, keep a cool head, and do what was necessary to get her back.

His car was low on petrol, so he drove into a service station and pulled up at a pump. Inside the shop there was only one till open and a longish queue had formed. When he was almost there, the man in front of him was having an argument with the woman operating the till. It was something to do with the man trying to use contactless, but the card machine wouldn't accept his card. The woman was trying to explain that his total bill was higher than the limit allowed for contactless. Barney was fuming. He was close to telling him to stop being such a prat and just put his card into the machine. After a long and pointless wait, he eventually paid up and got out of the way, allowing Barney to approach the window.

'What a pain in the arse he was.'

'I know. We get them like that now and again. How can I help?'

'Pump seven please.'

'There doesn't appear to be any sale on pump seven.'

Barney turned around and looked out of the window, then pointed.

'That's my car next to pump seven.'

'I know. But you haven't put any petrol in.'

'But I… Oh… Err …'

It then dawned on him that she was right. He had forgotten to put any petrol in.

He could hear some of the people in the rapidly increasing queue behind him making comments. He walked away as quickly as he could. He heard the woman say, 'We're getting all of the weirdos in here today.'

He got in his car and headed for the next petrol station feeling embarrassed. He had behaved in a way that he berated other people for behaving. He wondered if this would change his tolerance levels in future. Should he make more allowances for others who may have other things on their minds? What if their wives have been abducted too? What if they've just been told they've got cancer? What if their football team had just thrown away a three goal lead? He then promised to himself that he would try to be a bit more understanding, as unlikely that it was.

Six hours later, he met Mary outside the hospital.

'I'm not sure what you're hoping to get out of this. He's not capable of anything at the moment.'

'I know. But I'm getting desperate. Besides, I'm doing the decent thing by visiting him.'

Once again Bowles's wife was there.

'Hello Mary. What a nice surprise. I hope Richard is going to be a bit kinder to you this time. And who is this?'

'This is Barney, who used to work with Richard.'

'Oh my god! Not the infamous Cecil Barnard? My husband talked about you all the time. Far too often in fact.'

'Nothing bad I hope?', asked Barney.

'Yes. Mostly bad I'm afraid.'

Richard seemed a lot calmer than last time, although the bleeps on his machine appeared to get a little louder, and the lights flash faster when he saw who had come to visit him.

'Cecil. What a surprise. You're the last person I expected to visit.'

'I just wanted to see how you were.'

'I'm getting better. I hear you're back working with us.'

'I was. But I've had to quit again.'

That was a welcome snippet of information, and caused the bleeps and lights on the machine to slow down again. They all talked for an hour about nothing much. Richard apologised to

Mary for his behaviour to her on her previous visit, and thanked her for her efforts in keeping the company running in his absence. Barney tried to steer the conversation in a direction which might have led to some clues about Alison's abduction, but by now he knew it was a waste of time and Bowles had nothing to do with it. Outside, in the car park, they stopped at Mary's car.

'Sorry. That was completely pointless. I was barking up the wrong tree.'

'Don't worry about it. What are you going to do now? Are you driving straight home, or are you staying in a hotel?'

'I hadn't even thought that far ahead. I haven't booked anywhere yet. I've been driving all night and I'm shattered.'

'Why not come back to our place? I've got to go back to work, but you can go back for a shower and a kip if you want, and stay for the night? The three of us can go out for a few drinks and a Chinese or something. It might take your mind off things for a while. Or we can go over the events of that evening and see if any other clues crop up?'

'Yes, that sounds like a great idea. I'm starving.'

Barney went to Liam and Mary's place via a Primark where he picked up an unnecessarily cheap change of clothes and had the shower and brief sleep. He was disappointed that he had to rule out Richard Bowles from his enquiries, but realistically he never thought he was ever involved.

Later they were in the local pub. The mood was subdued, and no matter how much they tried to steer the conversation away from Alison's plight, they inevitably kept coming back to it.

Barney told them the whole story about the demand for

money he had received.

'I really don't know what to do. I've always thought it was wrong to give in to blackmailers and kidnappers. That if you pay them, it will just encourage more people to do the same. But it becomes difficult to think that way when you're the victim. I resent paying anything. Not because it would cause me any financial hardship, but because I don't see why this scumbag, whoever he is, should be getting rewarded for doing this.'

Mary tried to be sympathetic.

'I agree with you. But getting Alison back safely has to be the priority.'

'I know. But is this man serious when he says he will kill Alison? Or is it just a bluff? On the other hand, if I give him the money, is there any guarantee he will let her go? Also, he threatened to hurt her if I went to the police. But I'd already reported her missing to the police before he got in touch. He would know that too because it was mentioned on the news,'

'I wish I knew the answers. How long has he given you to pay?'

'He never gave a deadline. All he said was he would send me instructions soon.'

'I can't believe how evil some people can be.'

'There is something that concerns me. This creep not only knew all about my financial situation, but he knew other details such as my address, and he knew an awful lot of stuff about Alison. It's as if someone who knows me very well had been talking to him, or more disturbingly, the person behind all this could be someone who I think is a good friend.'

Liam gulped. Something just occurred to him.

'What's the matter love?', asked Mary.

'Nothing. The beer went down the wrong way.'

They left the pub and went to the Chinese restaurant. Liam was unusually quiet and wasn't joining in the conversation. Mary kept asking him if he was ok. He assured her he was. But later, when they had finished their food, he couldn't stay quiet any longer.

'I've got something to tell you. Do you remember that nerdy geezer called Kenneth who came to work for us, but didn't last long because he was useless?'

'Yes', they both said at the same time.

'Well, the two of us were talking in the canteen at work, and he was asking me all kinds of questions about you Barney. I didn't think there was any harm. I was just being friendly.'

'What sort of questions?'

'He tricked me into giving him your address. He said he wanted to send you a Christmas card.'

'In April?'

'Yes. Oh. I see what you mean. I didn't think of that. Not only that. I told him you were a millionaire. But worst of all he somehow got it out of me that Mary and Alison were going for a night out in London. He seemed to have an unhealthy obsession with Alison.'

'Why would that be?', said Barney. 'He'd never met her. He never knew her.'

Barney asked Mary, 'What else do you know about him? When he applied for the job, he must have given details, such as his full name, and where he lives.'

'I'll check it all when I get back to the office tomorrow.'

'All I know is, I found him a bit creepy. And he got offended when I called him Ken. I thought that was unusual.'

Liam casually chipped in, 'Not that unusual. Apparently, Alison's ex-husband insisted on people calling him Kenneth.'

'What!', Barney and Mary yelled at the same time.

'Alison's former husband was called Kenneth? How did you know that?'

'That's what she told me once. It just cropped up in conversation. We were talking about my dad who insisted on being called Thomas, and hated it when anyone called him Tom. Surely you know the name of your wife's ex?'

'No, I didn't. She always referred to him as 'my ex-husband'. Or 'that bastard'. I've never heard her use his name.'

Mary asked, 'Have you never seen a photo of him?'

'No. She burnt all photos of him on the day she got divorced and deleted any images of him from her phone. It was all part of her breaking free from her past and starting a new life.'

'Are we seriously thinking this Kenneth could be Alison's former husband?'

'It's looking that way.'

'What are you going to do now?'

'I'll have to drive back in the morning and tell all this to the police.'

Barney offered to pay the bill, but Mary insisted on paying their share. There was quite a bit of food left over and Barney asked the waiter for some containers to take it home with him. The other two were surprised.

Mary said, 'You don't behave like a typical millionaire.'

'It's not about money. I just don't like seeing good food go to waste.'

Liam saw an opportunity to get back in their good books with a joke.

'I know. You can tell by just looking at you.'

Barney wasn't in the mood to find it funny.

Mary asked, 'When are you going to eat it? You can keep it in our fridge overnight, but it's going to be in your car all the way home.'

'No, I'm intending having it for breakfast.'

Liam said, 'Yuk. Who has Chinese food for breakfast?'

'The Chinese do. Unless you think Beijing is full of English takeaways that do marmalade on toast, and Crunchy Nut Cornflakes? I have had this same conversation with Alison every time we go out for an Indian. I take the leftover curry and have it for breakfast. Do you think people in India only eat one meal a day, in the evening? Do they not have breakfast and lunch too?'

'Okay. Enjoy your Chinese breakfast. If you change your mind, I can cook your favourite breakfast.'

'What's my favourite breakfast?'

'Going by your previous visits, I would say fried eggs, bacon, sausages, black pudding, hash browns, baked beans, tomatoes, mushrooms, and toast.'

'You need to soak the beer up somehow.'

Liam was feeling ashamed.

'I'm really, really sorry. I was just trying to be friendly. I felt sorry for him. He'd just spent a day working with you Barney, and that's an ordeal for anyone. He sounded like he needed a friend. He said you didn't like him. I didn't think I was doing any harm.'

Barney said it was no problem, even though he didn't mean it. He was still in his being tolerant mode. Mary was less sympathetic.

'Oh Liam. As Bernard Manning used to say, if brains were dynamite, you wouldn't have enough to blow your hat off.'

'That's uncalled for. I'm not as stupid as you think. And I couldn't give a shit what the opinions are of someone who sells turkey burgers for a living.'

22

Alison sat in the hard wooden chair and reflected on her life. She could be forgiven for thinking she had been dealt a bad hand. Apart from the misfortune of bumping into this evil bastard at a bus stop and marrying him, she'd had a heart attack, and a scare about possibly losing her eyesight. On the other hand, she had a son who meant everything to her. If only she could be with him now. It didn't matter that he cut all his hair off. It didn't seem important anymore. She had married Barney, who she was missing terribly. She really loved him, but she gave him a hard time, and if ever she gets out of this, she will be so much nicer to him.

She had just returned from a bathroom visit. Her trips to the bathroom had been difficult and humiliating. He had forced her to get there using little jumps in an undignified manner because he wouldn't untie her legs. It all added to the loathing she felt towards him. If ever she got out of this alive, she was determined he was going to suffer. But was there any chance of that? She wasn't even sure if she wanted Barney to come up with the money. She was torn between getting away from this or letting Kenneth win. But something happened next which gave her a glimmer of hope.

She told him she needed a shower and a change of clothes.

'You can have a shower. I'm not a monster. I've even bought you some of the clothes you like.'

'They won't be clothes I like. They will be clothes you like. That was another way of you controlling me. I had to dress how you told me. It got to the point when the only clothes I enjoyed wearing were my work uniform.'

'You do realise that I will have to completely untie you if you are going to have a shower. I wouldn't want you to risk slipping over.'

'So?'

'I can't risk taking my eyes off you. If you aren't tied up, you might try to make a run for it. I will have to come in and watch you shower. And I'll be holding the cricket bat in case you try to do something stupid.'

The words made her skin crawl. How had she ever married this creep? It was a bit like that film 'Sliding Doors'. She had only missed the bus by two minutes. If she had managed to catch it, she would have never met Kenneth and her life would have taken a different path.

She had the shortest shower she had ever had in her life, with Kenneth watching, then he dragged her hands behind her back and tied the rope. But this time something felt different. She could move her hands a with a lot more freedom than before. He hadn't tied her up properly. Had he made his first mistake? She had to stay cool. If there was any chance of escape, she would have to time it perfectly.

'You should be happy Alison. Today I might have some news for you. I intend to give your husband the instructions for delivering my money. As long as he comes up with the money and doesn't try anything stupid, you could be free soon.'

'I'll be happy if he gives you nothing.

'That could be most unfortunate for you.'

'I don't care. I still hope he gives you nothing.'

'He can't think much of you if he won't pay up to get you back.'

'Oh right, and by comparison you were a model husband who showed me how much you thought of me by mentally torturing me until I was miserable and subservient.'

'I thought he was an arrogant prat, full of his own opinions, and judgemental of everyone else.'

'He's not perfect, but he's worth ten of you. He was the only one there for me when I had a heart attack, and when I had a scare about my eyesight. If I was still married to you at the time, you would no doubt have blamed me for those things. And you have the gall to call someone else judgemental. I'm going to enjoy watching you get your comeuppance. I might even come and visit you in prison, just so I can laugh in your face.'

'Sorry to disappoint you, but it's not going to happen.'

'Do you seriously believe you can get away with this? Even if he pays you, I know who you are. The police will easily hunt you down.'

'No, they won't. I've got it all planned. I will be a long way from here. They'll never find me. And it won't matter that you know me. I could make sure that you won't get the chance to tell them anything.'

'And if he doesn't pay? You can't keep me here forever.'

'I don't intend to. I would find somewhere else to dispose of you.'

Alison wanted to tell him she wasn't frightened by his threats.

That it was all just a bluff that he didn't have the bottle to carry out. But she thought it might be wiser to stay cool and work on the rope around her wrists after he left the room.

Kenneth not only left the room, but she also heard him leave the house. She didn't know how long he would be gone, but once she heard a car drive away, she got to work. He had indeed made a hash of tying her wrists, and she managed to wriggle free in ten minutes. After that it wasn't too difficult to untie the rope from her ankles. When she was free, she rushed around the house looking for a telephone, but couldn't find one. She slowly crept towards the front door and pushed it open.

Outside in the fresh air and daylight she blinked, and took in deep breaths. She wasn't aware of the person watching her from the other side of a fence. She looked around and realised she was in the middle of nowhere. What should she do next? Where could she go?

She told herself not to panic. She needed to stay cool and think carefully. She needed to make the right decision. What she did know deep down was the only sensible course of action was to run as far away and as fast as she could and get help from anyone she could.

But what she did next wasn't sensible at all. She didn't know why she did what she did. But something compelled her to do it. She went back inside the house and closed the door. All of this was being watched by the figure on the other side of the fence. Then she returned to the room which had been her prison cell for the past few days and sat back down in the chair.

23

Barney reported to the police station and asked for Sergeant Price, who eventually made his way to the reception desk.

'Ah. Good afternoon Mr Barnard. Come this way.'

Barney followed him to an interview room.

'Have you any further developments?'

'Yes I do', replied Barney. 'Do you?'

Price again ignored the provocation.

'I am still working on the case. No new evidence has come our way.'

'Fortunately, I'm having a bit more success than you. First of all, I have been contacted again this morning. He wants the money by tomorrow evening. In used notes. He had given details of the place to drop it. He says if it isn't there, or there is any indication that I have told the police, Alison will be killed.'

'Is it feasible to get the money ready that quickly?'

'I've got no idea. It's not something I've has to do before. But the question is irrelevant. I've decided not to pay him. I don't believe he will carry out his threat.'

'I see. Do you have any reason to think that?'

'No. Just a feeling. But my friends and I think that the kidnapper could be Alison's former husband.'

'I see. And what has happened to bring you to that

conclusion?'

Barney ran through the process that pointed them to Kenneth.

'My, you're quite the detective.'

'Yes. It's not that difficult when you're prepared to put in a bit of effort.'

At last Barney had made a comment that had visibly annoyed Price. He enjoyed the moment.

Price continued, despite his irritation.

'Tell me everything you know about this man.'

Barney went through everything he knew, which wasn't all that much. The details Mary had found on his job application were all fake, including his surname and address. He had been very clever at covering his tracks.

'What happens next Sergeant?'

'Leave it with me. I'll be in touch.'

'That is so reassuring', Barney muttered as he walked away. He left the police station, hardly brimming with confidence that Price would achieve anything.

He wasn't sure what he himself could achieve. He went home to think about it. He tried to convince himself he was doing the right thing in not giving the money. But what if Kenneth wasn't bluffing, and he did something horrible to Alison?

After an afternoon of ideas spinning around his head, he came up with a half-arsed plan. It wasn't even a plan at all. He would go to the arranged drop off point tomorrow night with a bag with no money in it and a weapon of some kind, and somehow try to turn the tables on Kenneth. Barney was no tough guy, but he'd fancy himself in a punch up with a weed like Kenneth. He had to try something.

24

Alison waited in the room that had become her prison cell. She was nervous, shaking, and breathing heavily. Questioning her own actions. She should have got away when she had the chance. But it was too late. She needed to stay strong, and keep a cool head. She heard a car pull up outside. Her heart was beating faster, and she was trembling. Then she heard the front door to the house open. She could hear Kenneth walking around the other room and making conversation with himself. But she knew it wouldn't be long before he came in to torment her again. She sat there waiting for what seemed an eternity, but was just over twenty minutes. Then she heard the door handle turning. Kenneth walked in to find the room in darkness. He tried the light switch, but it remained dark. He heard Alison call out.

'The main lightbulb blew just after you left. But the bedside lamp should work, only I can't get to it. Would you mind switching it on?'

Kenneth fumbled his way to the bedside and reached for the lamp. He found the switch and the room was illuminated once again. The first thing he saw was Alison standing in front of him holding the cricket bat. He laughed in her face.

'Don't be so ridiculous. Put that down. You aren't going to use it. You are weak. Very weak. You always did as I told you. And you are going to do what I tell you now. You know you will.'

If ever she needed any more incentive, that was it. She swung the bat with a ferocity fuelled by years of hatred for this man. But she missed! The momentum of the swing caused her to fall to her knees. But in dodging the bat, Kenneth swayed backwards and also fell to the ground. It didn't stop him taunting Alison.

'I knew you couldn't do it. Like I told you, you're weak and pathetic.'

They both scrambled to get to their feet, but Alison had the advantage. She'd only fallen to her knees, while Kenneth was sprawled out on the floor. Once she was up, she swung the bat again. This time Kenneth was in no position to get out of the way.

The blow crashed into his kneecaps with a sickening crunch, and he fell back down to the ground screaming.

She leaned over him and enjoyed his pain and yelled, 'Now, how would you like to be returned with two broken legs?'

Kenneth cried out in agony and begged for mercy, but Alison wasn't finished yet. She lifted the bat above her head and was about to smash it down on to Kenneth's head.

'You think I'm weak and pathetic, do you? Let's see how weak and pathetic you think this is.'

But because she was so focused on her target, she hadn't heard another car pull up outside and the door open again. She heard the voice.

'Okay, that's enough Mrs Barnard. Put the bat down and step away from him.'

Alison paused and held the bat above her head. She held the pose for a few tense moments, while the new arrivals looked on. They had no chance of reaching her in time to stop her. Kenneth trembled on the floor and waited for his fate. She still very much wanted to do it. But deep down she knew it wouldn't be the best course of action and she dropped the bat to the floor. Then she burst into tears. A female police officer led her to an armchair, sat her down and then made her a cup of tea. Sergeant Price went through the motions of arresting Kenneth, although he wasn't going anywhere without the help of an ambulance. Alison had done a proper job on his kneecaps.

Twenty minutes later, Barney ran through the door and Alison burst into yet more tears. They ran toward each other and were locked in an embrace for a few minutes before Sergeant Price interrupted their moment.

'You got here remarkably quick Mr Barnard. I hope you didn't break the speed limit driving here.'

'No. I most certainly didn't, Sergeant Prick.'

'My name is Price. And if you call me that again, you'll be the next to get arrested.'

'What would be the charge?'

'First degree being a pain in the arse.'

'My mum won't be very happy with you if you arrest me.'

'It's a chance I'm prepared to take. My Elizabeth will understand.'

'Your Elizabeth?

'Erm, that's not what I said. Or meant.'

'Yes it was. But it doesn't matter. I don't care what your relationship is with my mum. I'm just glad this is over and Alison is safe.'

'Absolutely. I got the case solved in the end. I always do.'

'Well done Inspector Morse. But it seems to me like Alison had already sorted it out herself.'

'Yes. She had. But if we had arrived a few seconds later, she could have been facing a serious charge. She was about to knock his head off. I can hopefully get away with putting down the smashed kneecaps as self-defence, but if she had cracked his skull open with a baseball bat while he…'

Barney interrupted.

'It was a cricket bat, Hercule.'

Price had to once again hide his irritation and continued.

'If she had cracked his skull open with a cri… with a bat while he was writhing around on the ground in agony, begging for mercy, I wouldn't have had any choice. I could have been arresting her for GBH, or even murder, albeit with diminished responsibility. As it is, you can take her home. But we will need to take a statement as soon as possible. Would you mind coming to the station tomorrow morning, Mrs Barnard?'

'Yes. Okay', replied Alison, in a low subdued tone. All she wanted to do was to get home and see Jack, with or without his blonde curly hair.

On the way out, Alison had one last look at Kenneth who was now getting treatment from the paramedics, but said nothing. Barney did.

'Bad luck Kenny.'

'Piss off Cecil.'

'Don't be like that. When you get out of prison, would you

mind limping down to the nearest DIY shop?'

'Why?'

'You owe me a packet of fuses.'

25

The following evening Barney, Alison, Liam, and Mary were in a pub in the lake district. Alison and Mary were drinking champagne, while Barney and Liam were on lager. Alison had been to the police station to give her statement. Now Liam and Mary wanted to know all the details. They had driven up this morning. They were eager to see Alison, as the pair of them had a slight feeling of guilt. They felt their actions were in a tenuous way to blame for Alison's abduction. Mary for not looking after her properly on their night out, and Liam for blabbing too much information to Kenneth. But Alison didn't see it that way. She reserved her anger for Barney over 'Barbergate'. He was going to suffer for that.

'That was awfully brave of you to go back into the cottage and wait for him', said Mary. 'I would have been out of there like a rat up a drainpipe.'

'Yes, you're right. I should have just run. I don't know what came over me. I was so full of anger that I wasn't thinking straight. It probably wasn't the greatest idea I have ever had. But at least this way I got to hurt that bastard. Now, not only will he go to prison, but he will go to prison in a lot of pain too.'

'I hope you didn't keep the cricket bat?', joked Barney.

'No, the police took it as evidence, but I can easily buy another one. We still have the matter of Jack's hair to discuss.'

Liam helped Barney out by intervening.

'That was pure genius taking the lightbulb out. I'd never have thought of that.

'Why thank you Liam. It just came to me. You could even say it was a lightbulb moment.'

They all laughed, even though Liam didn't know why he was laughing. But Mary wanted to continue with her questioning.

'What I don't understand is, why did the police turn up when they did?'

'Apparently, when I briefly went outside, a woman from the adjacent cottage was watching me from behind her fence. She recognised me from a photograph which had been shown on the local news. She phoned the police who came round immediately.'

'And how did you end up there, Barney?'

'Sergeant Prick called me when he was on his way there. He thought it would be helpful if I went there to see Alison. I doubt that would be normal protocol, but he's not the sort who would care about that. He's not so bad really.'

Alison didn't want to talk about it anymore. She changed the subject.

'How's things going at Vendetta?'

Mary told her, 'Things are not very good. Losing you and Barney for the week when you were going to work didn't help much. And we're going to lose Liam too. He's leaving at the end of the month. He got that job at the leisure centre. They called him with the job offer when he was in Istanbul. Sorry love. I mean Torquay. But Richard Bowles is improving, so hopefully he will come back soon and sort everything out.'

'Nice one Liam. Congratulations. I hope it all goes well for you', said Barney, desperately trying to steer the conversation away from the problems at Vendetta because he had an inkling that he knew what Alison was about to say. His inkling proved to be accurate.

Alison came up with the suggestion. 'If you think we could be of any use to you, the two of us can still help out next week?'

Barney wanted to protest, but held back. It was unlikely he could get out of it.

'That would be brilliant', said Mary. 'I'll see you on Monday morning. And this time turn up please.'

26

It was Sunday morning, and Barney wasn't in a good mood. He wanted to spend a few days at home doing the things he enjoyed doing most. Relaxing with a cold beer, watching television, listening to music, going for walks by the lake, and squirting the cats with the hosepipe. Not having to deal with rude and idiotic vending machine users. He toyed with the idea of pretending to be ill, but soon dismissed it. There was no way Alison was going to fall for that. He decided to try another strategy.

'Are you sure you want to do this?', he asked. 'I mean have you fully recovered from your ordeal? I'm worried about you.'

'I'm fine. You're just looking for excuses to get out of it.'

'I'm so sorry for being so caring.'

'Don't bullshit me. You just don't want to do it.'

'Okay. I admit it. I don't want to do it.'

'But you will.'

'You do realise it means mum will have to look after Jack for another week?'

'I'm prepared to take the risk. She might not let him paint the kitchen and the cat purple, or get drunk and fall asleep while he cuts his hair off, but I think she'll manage.'

'What about George and Mildred? Who will feed them?'

'I've already made arrangements for them. You must be really desperate to get out of it if you're trying to use phoney concern for the cats.'

It then occurred to Alison that she was being pushy, even though she had promised to herself during her captivity that she would try to be less bossy. She changed her tone.

'A wise man once told me it didn't matter how much money you had, good friends were the most valuable thing in your life.'

'Who said that? Confucius?

'No. His name was Cecil Barnard.'

'My Dad? It doesn't sound like something he'd say.'

'You don't fool me. It was you. You said those words to me at our wedding party.'

'I must have been drunk.'

'No, you weren't. Well, yes you were. But that's not the point. You were looking around at all your friends and there were tears in your eyes when you said it. I've never heard you say something you mean so much, and you're not the sort of man who holds back in saying things you mean.'

'OK. Just don't tell anyone.'

'I won't. Come on. Show a bit more enthusiasm. You were right when you said good friends were the most valuable thing in your life. Our friends need our help. It's only for a week and then you can retire for good. I promise.'

'Okay. You win. I can't say no to a good-looking girl like you.'

He pinched her bottom and she playfully slapped him on his face.

'Don't try any of your fake flattery on me. I won't fall for it. Anyway, once our little stint at Vendetta is over, we've got the trip to Cornwall to look forward to.'

'What? What do you mean? You aren't going to Cornwall. Are you?'

'I certainly am. It should be good. I've always wanted to go to Cornwall.'

'No, no, no, no, no. You can't. No.

'Yes, yes, yes, yes, yes. I can. Yes.

'How do you even know about it?'

'Roy phoned while you were still asleep. He had heard about me on the news and wanted to see if I was alright. Then he invited me to the Cornwall trip. I could hardly say no. Don't worry. I won't cramp your style. I've seen you drunk plenty of times. Unless you were planning to get up something naughty?'

'No. Of course I'm not. But it's a lad's thing.'

'No it's not. Fiona is going. And Tom is taking his girlfriend. I wouldn't want to go if I was the only female.'

'Terrific.'

Alison packed bags for herself and Jack, while Barney moped around, now in an even worse mood since Alison's announcement about Cornwall. When it was time to leave, Alison put some shoes on Jack and combed what was left of his hair.

'Come along my little darling. Let's say goodbye to the pussycats, then we'll drive to grandma's house.'

Barney was seething by now. On top of which, Alison had just come out with one of the things she knew would irritate him.

'Why do you tell him they're called pussycats? They're just cats! Why teach a young kid a word which isn't real, and is actually longer than the real word? Kids his age have enough real words to learn without filling their brains with this nonsense. When I was a kid, my grandma used to tell me about bunny rabbits. Then I got laughed at when I said it at school until I found out they were just called rabbits.'

'Oh, take no notice of grumpy daddy.'

Jack joined in.

'Ha ha. Daddy is grumpy.'

They dropped Jack off at Barney's mum's house and set off for the south once again. They used Barney's car. The van Alison was going to use had been recovered from the Dorchester hotel and she was going to pick it up from the Vendetta depot. Barney had made sure he got in first to book the hotel. Alison would rather have done it herself.

'I suppose you booked us into the grottiest, cheapest hotel you could find?'

'Not at all. It's perfectly reasonable. I stayed there on my previous visit.'

'Wasn't that a Travelodge?'

'I don't think so. I can't remember. But it was perfectly comfortable. And that's another thing. If you insist on coming to Cornwall, we're staying in the same hotel as all the others. No going off looking for a Ritz or something,'

'Roy has already booked a place in Penzance. And it's not really a hotel. It's more like a bed and breakfast. A bit like your mum's place. It's very nice. But it's not the cheapest. Don't forget, everyone else going are also millionaires now. And they're not meanies like you.'

'I'm not a meanie. I just don't believe in wasting money when it isn't necessary. Everybody is going to be so pissed it hardly matters what the quality of the hotel is. We could all sleep on a pile of broken glass and barbed wire, and none of us would notice.'

'Look at it this way. We've now got a quarter of a million pounds we might not have had.'

'What do you mean?'

'I'm talking about the ransom money for my release.'

'Ah. That money.'

'Yes. That money. I'm so glad he didn't get it. As a matter of fact, I was secretly hoping you weren't going to pay him.'

'That's good. Because I wasn't going to.'

'What? You were going to just leave me there and let me suffer the consequences? You bastard!'

'But you just said… '

'Never mind what I just said. You were going to just abandon me?'

'You're damned if you do, you're damned if you don't. As someone famous once said.'

'Eleanor Roosevelt.'

'I thought it was Bart Simpson.'

Several hours later they arrived at the Travelodge in Winchester.

27

Mary decided the most productive use for Barney on Monday was to go around with some of the new trainees. Barney wasn't happy with this. His previous attempt in this role hadn't worked out great. He would much rather just work on his own, but couldn't be bothered to argue about it, so he reluctantly accepted things. On Monday he accompanied a young man called Carl for the day, passing on the benefits of his dubious wisdom. It turned out not to be as bad as he was expecting, as the lad had liked football and cricket, and had similar political views to him, so they had plenty to talk about. His taste in music was not to Barney's liking though, just like most people of that age, so he had to take charge of what they listened to in the car.

They completed three fairly easy calls. The fourth one should have also been easy, but was made unnecessarily difficult by a third party. One of the company rules was that it was the responsibility of the engineer to find out the part number of anything that was needed to repair the machine. He felt this often wasted a lot of time that could have been used more productively. During his working days, he would have a large range of traditional paper manuals and could just look up the part numbers. But he no longer had any. He burnt them all in a mini bonfire soon after he had won the lottery and cracked open a bottle of champagne while he watched them go up in flames. In the four years since he retired, they had been using a different system. All the parts manuals were now on an app. But he didn't have that either. His only option was to call the machine manufacturers. From past experience, he remembered some of them were friendly and helpful. Some of them talked to you like you were an idiot. The company he needed to contact were called Brewalot. Barney had no choice but to ring them.

'Good morning. You're through to the Brewalot technical help department. How can I help you?'

'Hi. I'm calling to see if you could help me with a part number?'

'Who are you. And which company do you work for?'

'I am Cecil Barnard. And I work for Vendetta.'

'Don't you have the app? All Vendetta engineers should have the app. It was part of an agreement we had with you.'

'I don't know about any agreement. I'm only working temporarily. And I need this part.'

'Tch! What is the part called?'

'I don't know what it's called, but I can describe it.'

'Tch! Okay. Describe it.'

'It's the nozzle where the drinks come out.'

'What sort of machine are we talking about?'

'It's called an Exotica.'

'What model?'

'I don't know. But I believe the part is the same for all the Exotica models.'

'What part do you need?'

'It's the nozzle where the drinks come out. Still.'

'I don't know what you mean.'

'The drinks, such as coffee and tea come out. There's a black plastic nozzle. That.'

'I'm still not sure what you mean. You'll have to describe it better than that.'

'When a user places their cup in the machine to get a drink, directly above it is a black plastic item which I would describe as a nozzle. You probably have another name for it. But if my description is too confusing for you, I would suggest you pass the telephone to the nearest grown up and I'll see if I can have more luck with them. Is your mummy at home?'

The call went dead. The Brewalot man had obviously taken offence. Not that Barney was bothered in the slightest.

The incident provided an opportunity to teach Carl an important lesson. He attempted to drum into him the importance of not taking any shit from anyone. With a bit of luck, he had helped create another rebel.

Carl had been okay to work with. Tuesday's companion would prove to be a bit more challenging.

On Tuesday morning he picked up Bill, yet another new trainee. Mary wanted him to drive to west London to clear up four long overdue jobs and assess Bill's potential while he was at it. That didn't take him very long. The man was as thick as mince, and clearly had no engineering experience. He wondered where they were getting these people from. There was a shortage of experienced engineers, and the job centre were sending anybody to them out of desperation.

Despite his shortcomings, Bill seemed an okay guy, so Barney tolerated him while completing the first three jobs, successfully. For the fourth job, the reported fault was that the cups weren't dropping, but call Colin for more information. This filled Barney with dread. In his opinion, Colin was the most boring person in the world. He hated it when Colin phoned him and used to pretend he was in a lift and lost the signal. Colin could be forgiven for thinking that Barney lived in a lift. Reluctantly he phoned him.

'Hello Barn. How's it going? It's been a long time. I heard you were back.'

'Yes. Four years. It seems like yesterday.'

'Let me tell you what I've been up to. Honestly, you wouldn't believe it…'

'Maybe later Colin. I'm about to go in a lift. I just called to ask you about this machine that doesn't drop cups. It says call you for more information.'

'Yes. I ordered a new cup drop unit and apparently it has been delivered to site directly. It should be at the goods inward. Interestingly enough I did a job this morning you might want to hear about …'

'Sorry Colin. I have to go. The lift has arrived. Thanks for your help. We'll catch up later.'

They drove to the site and Barney paid for an hour parking. With hindsight he should have paid for two hours, but parking in London was so expensive, and despite his wealth, he still resented wasting money. Changing a cup unit should only take about twenty minutes. But it took half an hour to locate the unit. It wasn't at goods inward. But the remaining half hour should still be enough to complete the job. The cup unit was linked to the machine via a twelve pin plug and was held on by four screws. The cable was secured with cable ties.

'Bill, I desperately need a visit to the gents. It would save time if you would remove the old cup drop unit. There are a pair of wire cutters in my tool bag. You will need them.'

Barney went to the toilet, and was in for a shock when he returned. He surveyed the scene and couldn't believe what he was seeing.

'What the fuck have you done?'

'I cut the cup unit out like you said.'

'The cutters were to remove the cable ties. Not to cut through the fucking cable. We are going to need that cable to attach to the new unit. It's going to take me hours to put that right. That's twelve wires to repair. What a nightmare.'

'Oh. Sorry I misunderstood what you wanted me to do.'

Barney was furious. He really wanted to have a go at him. Even someone with no engineering experience shouldn't have done something so stupid. But it wouldn't have done much good. The man clearly wasn't suitable for the job. Barney just needed to get away from him for a moment.

'Our parking time will run out before I can repair this. I'll start doing it if you would go and move the car.'

'Why does it need to be moved. Can't I just put some more money in?'

'No. That isn't allowed. I would get a fine. You have to move it to a different bay. When you've done that, put two hours on it. Hopefully that will be long enough to put right the destruction you have caused.'

Bill went out to do as he was asked, Barney set to work rectifying the damage. It went as well as could be expected, and he had the machine up and running in an hour and twenty minutes. Bill was feeling embarrassed.

'I'm really sorry about that.'

'It's alright. No harm done. Let's get to the car and head back to Winchester,'

Barney followed Bill to where he had parked the car. Or to where Bill had thought he had parked the car.'

'It's gone!'

'What do you mean it's gone?'

'The car. It's not here.'

'Are you sure this is where you left it?'

'Yes, I am sure. Unless it was the next street.'

They had a good look around, but couldn't find it. Had it been stolen? He thought about calling the police. Then he remembered someone telling him about an app called TRACE, which was for locating cars that had been towed away for parking illegally. Using it, he discovered that his car had been towed to a pound at Chelsea Harbour. He was struggling to keep his cool. He was on the verge of thumping Bill. They took the tube, Barney not saying a word, while Bill maintained an embarrassed silence. When they arrived, an arrogant official explained that the car had been parked on a blue badge bay, reserved for disabled drivers. There would be a penalty charge of £160, reduced to £80 if paid within fourteen days, and a release fee of £200. Barney paid the money, went to the car, climbed in and drove off still not saying a word.

Back at the office, Mary was packing away her stuff and was looking forward to going home following another hard day. She just wanted to see Liam and Louis, have a shower and watch some lowbrow television. Then her phone rang. It was unusual to get any calls this late in the day. Reluctantly she picked up the phone.

'Hello. You're through to Vendetta. How can I help you?'

'Hello Mary. It's Bill. I'm stranded in London and I don't have enough money to catch a train.'

'Where's Barney?'

'He wouldn't let me in the car. He just drove off and left me here.'

'Oh for fucks sake.'

28

On Wednesday morning, Barney and Liam were teamed up again. There was a crisis that needed some diplomacy, and Mary inexplicably thought Barney was the man for the occasion, despite the mood he was in because of the things that happened yesterday. Mary wasn't in a great mood either. She had got home an hour later than usual the previous evening because she had to work out a way to get Bill back from London. Eventually she had managed to buy him a train ticket on the internet, but it took ages, and she wasn't very happy with Barney. Not for the first time. On the plus side, she could safely assume that Bill wasn't up to the job and could tell him his services were no longer required.

They were sent to Southampton to a shop belonging to a small supermarket chain. They were moving to a new location and needed two vending machines taking from the old site to the new one. Mary had the decency to warn them the man who they had to deal with, someone called Gary, was in a foul mood on the phone. Barney wasn't too bothered. He'd heard it all before. On arrival, it became obvious that the Gary's mood had not improved. He was straight on the warpath.

'These machines were supposed to be moved last week. We were meant to vacate the premises three days ago, but your machines are still here. What is going on?'

Barney, as he always used to in his heyday started off in a calm manner.

'I honestly don't know mate. I wasn't working here last week. All I can do is get them moved today.'

'Don't I even get an explanation, or an apology?'

'Nah. Not from me. I'm here to do a job, not apologise for someone else's cock up. I would suggest you call the people you pay the money to if you want an explanation.'

'I don't like you attitude.'

'Ahh. That brings back memories. You don't like my attitude. If I had a penny for every time someone said that to me, I'd have £3.64.'

Thankfully Gary's phone rang, and he wandered away to answer it.

The problem with moving machines from one location to another was that they had to deal with the logistics team. Logistics were made up of pairs, who had cruelly been given nicknames by the rest of the staff, such as Little and Large, or the Chuckle Brothers. Barney didn't know who he would be getting today. But desperately hoped it wasn't going to be Laurel and Hardy. The last time he had the pleasure of their company was when they were doing a machine uplift from a hotel near Heathrow airport, and it resulted in them parking their lorry in front of the airport shuttle bus so it couldn't move, and then losing the lorry keys, causing chaos among people trying to catch their flights.

But whoever was coming, they hadn't arrived at the agreed time, so Barney called Mary.

'Hello gorgeous. Have you cheered up since this morning?'

'Hello dickhead.'

'That would be a no then.'

'What do you want? No, let me guess. You have abandoned

someone else in the middle of nowhere?'

'He's lucky that's all I did to him. Have you any idea how much money that gormless twat cost me?'

'Just don't tell me this job is another balls up.'

'Not yet. But there's still time. Logistics haven't arrived yet. I need to give them a call to find out where they are. Who is down to do the job?'

'Bill and Ben.'

'Oh great. That's all I need. The flowerpot men.'

'Flobadob', said Mary.

'Yeah, and a floba fucking dob to you too.'

Barney phoned the Flowerpot Men and found out they had been sitting outside in their lorry for twenty minutes, for no particular reason. It wasn't a promising start. They came into the building following the suggestion from Barney. He was already getting agitated with them, and he hadn't even met them yet.

'Okay. Liam is un-plumbing the machines. Can we get them onto the lorry as quickly as possible so we can get this guy off our backs?'

'Yes guv. No sweat.'

When Liam had finished, Bill and Ben wheeled the pump truck underneath the first machine and manoeuvred it towards the door, but then stopped.

'We've got a problem guv. The machine won't fit through the door.'

Barney got his tape measure out of his tool bag and measured the doorway. At this point Gary returned and wasn't pleased to hear the news. Barney tried to fight back.

'The machines obviously didn't come in through this door. Have there been any alterations made?'

'Yes. This wall was rebuilt three years ago.'

'That's hardly our fault.'

'Yes it is. You sent one of your engineers here two weeks ago to do what he referred to as a site survey. I wasn't here, but he sent me an Email saying there would be no problems getting the machines out. If he'd told us the door was too narrow, we could at least have had a chance to do something about it.'

Barney for once was lost for words. This was one of those situations when the irate customer had a point. Gary's phone temporarily came to the rescue again and he wandered away. Barney turned to Liam.

'Have you any idea who did the site survey? Whoever did it made a right cock up.'

'It was me.'

'You?'

'Yes. It was me.'

'Did you not measure the doorway? And the machine?'

'Yes. I did.'

'But the doorway is only 28 inches. The machine is 30 inches on its shortest side.'

'Ah, but I used centimetres. That must be where it went

wrong.'

'I... but... What? What are you... How can... Oh for...'

Barney had to bite his tongue. He didn't want to fall out with his friend. Gary returned and was understandably angry.

'This is completely unacceptable. What are you going to do about it?'

'There is only one solution that I can suggest. You'll have to knock part of your new wall down.'

'No. That's not an option.'

'In which case I have nothing left to offer. While I accept our engineer made a mess of the measuring, even if he had got it right and told you the machine wouldn't go through the door, you would still have been in the same position as you are now. The bottom line is, you did the alterations to the wall. In my book that makes it your own fault. Perhaps you ought to give me an apology.

29

On Thursday morning in the Winchester Travelodge, Alison was getting ready for work. Barney was still in bed. He didn't want to get up, but he kept telling himself he just had two more days to get through. Yesterday had been a stark reminder of some of the more frustrating moments he had regularly endured over the years. Only the thought of breakfast was what finally got him moving. The two of them made their way down to the restaurant, where Alison helped herself to cereal and fruit juice and Barney went for a large fry up and enough cups of tea to cause a shortage in China. He told her the tale of the fiasco yesterday, then asked her what she'd been up to.

'I've just been doing what I always did. Cleaning and filling vending machines. It's frustrating, because some of the machines have been empty for days because of staff shortages, and the customers are moaning a lot.'

'Yes, that sounds familiar. I think I'm just doing routine repairs today. I'm hoping to finish early. I'm going into London this evening to play in the darts match. Do you want to come?'

'No. I'll give this one a miss. I'll probably be working quite late, so I'll just stay in, read my book and have an early night. Try not to make any noise and wake me up when you're stumbling around drunk in the dark at midnight.'

'I'll do my best.'

The day was relatively uneventful for both of them. He had one particularly ludicrous job, which served as yet another reminder why he was glad to be retiring. He had been sent to a cold water dispenser, with the reported fault 'water splashing everywhere'. He was led to the machine by a man who pressed the button for cold water.

'See what I mean. It splashes everywhere.'

'You're meant to put a cup under it.'

'Not everybody does that.'

'Why would anyone press the button without putting a cup in place?'

'Some people like to run a bit of water out before they place their cup.'

'They shouldn't do that.'

'Why not?'

'Because it results in water splashing everywhere.'

'What can I do about it?'

'You could tell people to put a cup in place first. There's nothing wrong with your machine, so stop wasting my time. And don't forget to tell me you don't like my attitude.'

'Quite frankly I don't.'

'That's a relief. I was worried for a minute.'

He finished early and caught a train into Waterloo station in London, then a tube to Moorgate. The Mickey Mouse Club had a home match against Johnson and Smith, the most miserable and unfriendly team in the league. Nobody enjoyed playing against them. They took it far too seriously, and weren't gracious in defeat. They weren't all that gracious when they won either. They continually complained about everything. The lights weren't bright enough, the dartboard wasn't at the correct height, or the sandwiches were horrible.

When Barney walked into the Black Cat, he wasn't surprised to find Tom and Daffy already in there. They were always first there and had already had a few. He bought himself a beer and joined them. With these two, the conversation was always either football or real ale. If it was real ale, his mind would switch off completely. He could never understand how people could talk for so long about beer. On the other hand, if they were talking football, he would chip in with his opinions. Everyone in the team supported a different football team, which made for some very interesting conversations. As it turned out, they were talking politics, which Barney tried to avoid. He had strong opinions which not everyone agreed with. But on his arrival, they changed the subject. All they wanted to talk about was Alison's kidnapping. He was going to be telling the tale over and over again this evening. When the others arrived, he would have to go over it all again. He would rather just forget about it and get on with the darts, but that wasn't going to happen. First, he had to repeat everything to Roy, and then again to Fiona.

Eventually the match got under way. Johnson and Smith, taking it as seriously as ever took a 3-1 lead after the team leg and pairs. Then Mickey Mouse Club lost the first two singles and were 5-1 down when Barney came to play his singles match. He was up against a player nobody liked. He was a good player, but unfriendly and arrogant. Barney got off to a flyer, hitting 100 followed by a 140. This took his opponent by surprise, and he didn't like it. As he walked to the oche for his next shot, he paused and turned to Barney.

'Will you stop clicking your darts together?'

'What are you on about?'

'You're deliberately clicking your darts together trying to put me off.'

'Don't be so fucking stupid. I'm not doing anything. You just don't like losing.'

'I don't like losing to a cheat.'

That remark sent Barney over the edge. He squared up to his opponent and stared at him in the face. He looked as if he was about to swing a punch at him. Players from both teams stepped in and separated them. Following a few minutes of chaos and arguments, with a bit of shoving too, the game was eventually resumed. Barney had never wanted to win a game more in his life. But he played with a deadpan expression on his face. He had to appear not to be bothered by it all in case he lost. Much to his relief he didn't lose, nailing a first dart double eight. As the dart went in, he gave no reaction at all. He just stood still, turned his back on his opponent and said nothing. If this git was going to bury his pride and shake hands, he would have to come to Barney. Which he didn't.

Fiona thought it would be sensible to take Barney away from the heat of the situation. They sat down and chatted for a while, just the two of them. Fiona was always calm. She'd often had to deal with uncomplimentary comments about female darts players from ignorant men, but usually dealt with them by just beating them. She managed to calm him down, and they chatted about other things. The subject of the Cornwall trip came up. Barney was curious to know how many of the teams were taking their partners. He already knew Tom was taking his girlfriend. It suddenly occurred to him that he didn't know if Fiona was single, or married, or whatever. He had known her for a long time, and really ought to have known. But he clumsily asked the question.

'Are you taking anyone with you to Cornwall? Do you have a husband or a boyfriend?'

Her response wasn't what he was expecting. She mumbled a very quiet reply and looked visibly offended. More than offended. Her reaction suggested he had said something horrible to her.

'No, I don't.'

On the train back to Winchester that evening, all kinds of thoughts were running through his head. Why did the question upset her? Was there something he was missing here? Perhaps she was happily married and was just annoyed that Barney didn't know after all this time. Or she could have been through a messy divorce. Or it could even have been something more tragic. What if she'd had a boyfriend that was killed in a traffic accident or something. Surely he would have already heard if it was something like that. But he felt terribly guilty. He would make the effort to talk to her in Cornwall and find out what he'd said wrong, and at least get a chance to apologise to her.

30

Getting out of bed on Friday morning was even more difficult than the previous day, for Barney at least. Alison managed okay. She'd had a quiet night in and had a good long sleep. She wasn't even woken up when Barney stumbled around just after midnight, yelping in pain when he kicked his toe against the bed leg, and singing 'the Winner Takes it All', celebrating his darts victory over his awful opponent, louder than he realised while having a shower. It didn't help that he didn't feel hungry, so breakfast wasn't the motivation it usually was. As was often the case during his long career, all he wanted to do every Friday was to get through the day without any hassle from anyone, then go home. This was going to be his last ever Friday working, and there he was going to get one final reminder of why he was happy to never do it again.

Most of the day went exactly how he would have liked it. Easy fixes and relatively happy punters. But mid-way through the afternoon he was sent to an office, with the intriguing fault description of 'drink quality issue'. He was told to ask for Claire, who would explain the Issue. Claire had temporarily left the office when he arrived, but the reception let him check the machine, which he did, thoroughly as she didn't appear for another fifty minutes. She seemed pleasant enough when she introduced herself.

'Hi, I'm Claire. Have you solved our problem?'

'No. I'm not sure what the problem is. I was told that you had drink quality issues, but I can't find anything wrong, and I've tried every drink.'

'But I told them about the problem on the phone.'

'Sometimes I don't always get the complete information. Perhaps you should tell me.'

'The soup doesn't taste very nice.'

Barney vended a soup and took a drink.

'That tastes fine to me.'

'I know. It tastes fine to me too, but one of the directors on the second floor says he doesn't like it. And he's a very important man.'

'Vending machines don't discriminate. They treat important people in the same way as the rest of us peasants.'

'Can you check it all the same?'

'I already have. The mains water has a filter on it. The filter is in date. The boiler is clean. It supplies water for all the drinks, so if there was anything wrong with the water, none of the drinks would taste very nice. The soup mixing bowl is clean. The soup in the cannister is in date. It is a major brand. There is no reason for it to have a taste problem.'

'He says it is too salty. It's not as nice as the tins of soup he has at home.'

'Oh, so you're basically saying it's nothing to do with the actual vending machine. He just doesn't like the flavour of the soup. There's not a lot I can do about that. We don't make it. I can't change the recipe. You could try sending an Email to Batchelors. You never know. They may be persuaded to change the recipe of their very popular soup because one company director doesn't like it.'

'Do you think they will?'

'Err... No. I don't think they will. I have to confess I was being sarcastic. Not for the first time in my career, but most certainly the last.'

'What shall I tell him then?'

'Tell him not to drink the soup. Suggest he puts a tin of soup in a thermos flask and bring that in.'

'He won't like that.'

'I won't be able to sleep tonight.'

'Why not?'

'Oops. There I go again. I think I ought to leave now.'

He was relieved to get out of the building. It was by no means the worst encounter he had ever had, but the typically ludicrous nature of the visit was a fitting end to his working life.

After work they got together with Mary and Liam for a drink and a visit to an Indian restaurant. Mary thanked them for their help in her own inimitable style.

'You two have been most helpful, and I'm very fucking grateful.'

'No problem', said Barney, 'and don't forget, if ever you need any help again, any time of the day or night, just pick up the phone and call some other mug.'

'Cheers. I'm going to miss you, dickhead,'

Their contribution really had helped. Mary had things under control at work and would be delighted to hand back control to Richard Bowles when he returned next week. Bowles would be happy that Barney wasn't there anymore. Liam was even happier. He had only two more weeks in the job he wasn't any good at before embarking on his new career. Barney was happiest of all. He really was going to retire this time.

The following morning, the aftermath of far too many drinks made the drive back a tough one. At least for Barney it was. Alison slept for most of the way. They had to leave early to collect Jack from his mum. She had to go somewhere in the afternoon, no doubt some church related thing possibly involving his favourite police officer, which meant they had to leave a lot earlier than they would have ideally liked. It wasn't too bad a journey as far as traffic was concerned. It helped that Alison was asleep for most of the way. Barney spent the journey plotting revenge on the cat who mutilated his penis. The hosepipe drenching wouldn't work. They had sussed him out. As soon as he picked up the hose to water the plants, both cats scurried away and hid before he could even reach the tap. He had experimented with playing cat meows on YouTube on his phone, which at first caused some minor distress for Mildred, but she was now wise to that too it and wasn't concerned by it any longer. He'd even tried barking dogs, but this didn't bother her at all. She had never met any dogs. He needed something more effective.

They eventually arrived to collect Jack, and predictably Alison was all over him like a rash.

'How's my little darling? Have you been a good boy for grandma?'

'Oh yes. He's been lovely', gushed Elizabeth.

Barney was already suffering from a queasy stomach, and this wasn't helping matters. He just wanted to get home and have a rest. Unfortunately for him, Alison went straight upstairs for another sleep which meant he was watching Jack again. He felt that was grossly unfair. He had done all that driving while she slept. It should be him that was going for a lie down. He wasn't going to win. But if he was entrusted with looking after Jack, he would have to be vigilant from now on and make sure there were no more painting or haircut mishaps. He opted for doing the crossword in his newspaper instead. But to do so he needed a pen.

To Barney, one of the great mysteries in life was where all the pens went. He could buy a pack of a hundred, and they would all have vanished within days. He rummaged around in various drawers but couldn't find one. But he did find something else. It was a party popper which must have been left over from Christmas. He put it in his pocket. He thought it might come in handy sometime. He could take it to the darts next time they were playing Johnson and Smith and set it off just as the opponent who accused him of cheating was about to take his throw.

Before she disappeared upstairs, Alison had told him to feed the cats. He was reluctant to do it because they showed such little gratitude. George was unusually friendly and rubbed against his legs. Mildred hissed at him, but still ate the food.'

'You bloody hypocrite. You can hiss all you like. Revenge will be mine.'

Then he gave an evil laugh, like a master criminal in an old horror movie.

Half an hour later his big chance came. Both cats, as they always did, followed their feast with a sleep. George liked to sleep in cardboard boxes for some reason, and had found his favourite one. Mildred was curled up in an armchair. He looked at her for a while. He had to admit she was a beautiful cat. She looked so peaceful and content. How could anyone even think of disturbing her? No. He couldn't do it. Then he thought about himself curled up in bed that night, also probably looking beautiful and peaceful and content. Had the cat stopped and thought, 'No, I can't do it. I can't stick my claws into that dangly thing'? No. She just went ahead with her vicious assault. But even with the painful memory in his head, he still couldn't bring himself to disturb the beautiful little cat curled up in a ball, so blissfully.

Yes he could. He pulled the string on the party popper as close to her ears as he could get. She jumped out of her skin and moved so quickly he didn't even see it happen. It was as if she had just turned invisible.

'Now see how you like it', he cackled.

A few hours later, Alison was up and about and expressed some concern for the way Mildred was behaving. George was still asleep in his cardboard box, but Mildred was cowering in a corner under the kitchen table.

'Have you any idea what's up with Mildred? She looks terrified. You haven't been nasty to her, have you?'

'No. I haven't. And I resent the suggestion. All I did was feed them. They seemed okay. Then they went to sleep.'

'Okay. I'll let you off. But I wonder why she's acting so oddly. I've never seen her like this before.'

'I don't know. Maybe there was a dog barking outside that spooked her or something.'

But his butter wouldn't melt in my mouth act was about to backfire. Suddenly, Jack appeared from nowhere. Alison greeted him in customary fashion.

'Hello my little prince. How are you?'

Jack started whimpering.

'What's wrong my love?'

'Daddy made a loud bang and frightened the pussycat.'

31

Alison had made Barney suffer for his treatment of Mildred, despite her intention to be nicer to him. But when it came to the cats, or Jack, he wasn't going to get away with much. She'd just about forgiven him by the time the excursion to Cornwall arrived two weeks later. Alison suggested, or insisted would be a more accurate description, that they fly to Cornwall. There were flights from Manchester to Newquay. Barney was initially against it, but he didn't fancy the long, slow drive much, and when he looked at how short the flight was, he pretended to give in to her. They wouldn't need the car either. There was going to be a lot of drinking, so everyone would be travelling around on buses or in taxis.

Barney made a half- hearted attempt at rebuilding bridges concerning George and Mildred.

'I've arranged with one of the neighbours to feed the cats.'

'That's good of you. You owe them that much at least. Mildred still has PTSD thanks to you.'

'And I've got a big scar on my willy, thanks to her.'

'You'd better not be so cruel when we get a dog.'

'No. I think I… Whoa! What did you just say?

'I want to get a dog.'

'Over my dead body.'

'Works for me.'

'You know how much I dislike dogs.'

'What have you got against dogs?'

'They are disgusting creatures. They are the slobs of the animal world. Imagine a man lazing about on a sofa in underpants he's been wearing for a fortnight, belching, farting, picking his nose, and scratching his armpits. He is the human equivalent of a dog. And he doesn't even go around sniffing other men's backsides.'

'Rubbish. Dogs are lovely.'

'Tell that to the next poor kid who gets half his face ripped off by one of them.'

'You can't judge them all by a few bad ones. They are loyal and intelligent creatures.'

'They are only intelligent compared to the people that own them. I've lost count of the number of times I've been walking along minding my own business, when one of these hideous animals has come charging menacingly towards me snarling and barking, and some cretin without two braincells to rub together tells me it's just being friendly and saying hello. These people seem oblivious that some people, such as me, are nervous around dogs. They have this delusion that everyone else in the world loves their dog as much as they do. There is no way a dog and I are going to live in the same house.'

'Alright. You win. I didn't realise how you felt. I won't make you live in the same house as a dog.'

'Thank you. You've got a hidden kind side after all.'

'I do. And I'll miss you. Will you come back and visit us?'

'Very well hidden in fact. You really would replace me with a dog?'

'Why not? He could sleep on the end of my bed. At least he wouldn't be snoring all night. And I could probably train him to put up those shelves that you've been promising to put up for the last six months.'

The flights went smoothly, and they arrived at the bed and breakfast in Penzance in time for the rendezvous in its pleasant little bar. It was run by a Mrs Brown, who was a stereotypical guest house landlady you would see in a bad sitcom forty years ago. She explained a few house rules, and they would have to be on their best behaviour during their stay. They gave her the nickname Eva. When they all were gathered, Barney realised how ridiculous his claim had been that the outing was a lad's thing. There were four men, Barney, Tom, Daffy, and Roy and three women, Alison, Fiona, and Tom's girlfriend Cheryl.

That evening they played the prearranged darts match against a pub team in Penzance. It was played in good spirit against a great bunch of characters. There were no dart clicking controversies or anything else like that. Nobody cared who won. The girls were made to play. They weren't given any choice. Fiona was already the best player in the team, but Cheryl and Alison did alright and enjoyed themselves immensely. Alison had never thrown a dart in her life, and wondered what all the fuss was about.

The next day they had a trip to the north coast to a place called Perranporth. Some of the darts players from the previous evening had recommended a pub called the Watering Hole. It didn't disappoint. It was located on a sandy beach, and Barney, with his love of drinking by the sea, thought it was the best pub he'd ever been in. They had a long, relaxed lunch with plenty of drinks.

Alison was sitting next to Cheryl and had the chance to get to know her. Tom had never brought along a girl to any of the darts matches or curry nights in all the years they had known him. He had never had much success with girls. More than one of them were thinking he was punching above his weight. How did he end up with someone so hot? Some cynics might even suggest that his two million quid share of the lottery win could have in some way increased his attractiveness.

The drunkenness was going to continue well into the evening. They had returned to the B&B in Penzance and a rendezvous back in the bar was suggested by Roy, who as ever was making sure some kind of schedule was being adhered to. It helped a lot, because without it, people would be wandering off all over the place and there would be chaos. Or so Roy kept telling them.

Most of the group, including Alison, went back to their rooms to freshen up, Barney opted not to. If he went back to the room, he would probably lie down on his bed while Alison was refreshing her makeup and getting changed, then fallen asleep and woken up feeling like shit. He went to the bar instead and ordered a pint. Much to his surprise, he found Fiona sitting in the bar on her own. She looked a little sad. He thought it would be a good opportunity to clear up the little misunderstanding he had with her two weeks ago.

'Hi Fiona, how's it going?'

'Fine', she replied rather abruptly.

'I'm glad I've got the chance to talk to you. There's something I'd like to ask you. If you don't mind?'

'Whatever.'

Barney had no idea what he'd said to upset her so much. But clearly from her reaction, whatever it was, she had not forgotten it.

'At the last darts match we were chatting. I asked you if you had a boyfriend or husband. You seemed upset that I asked. I'm sorry if I offended you in some way.'

'You didn't offend me.'

'Right. I'm glad I didn't.'

'Well no. Yes, you did offend me. You offended me a lot.'

'I am so sorry. That's the last thing I would want to do. You've always been a very good friend to me. What did I say that hurt you?'

'I don't have a husband or boyfriend. There's only one man I want.'

'Oh. Who might that be?'

'You.'

Barney had a mouthful of beer which spluttered all over his shirt. He would have to go to his room and get changed after all.

'Me? But…'

'I've always wanted to be with you. You must have known that?'

'No. I…'

'I was devastated when you got married. That was the day my dreams ended.'

'I had no idea you felt this way. If only I'd known. Things

could have been different. Why didn't you say something sooner?'

'You must have seen the signals?'

'No. I didn't see any signals. You did kiss me once, but I thought that was because I hit double sixteen in our pairs match. And because you'd had too much wine.'

'No. It was because I love you.'

'Oh. Err… I see that now. I… Err… I…'

'It's not too late. Come back to my room. We could make love, just one time.'

'I'm so sorry. It's too late. I'm a married man now, and my wife is here. It can't be.'

Fiona held his hand, leaned over and started kissing him. He felt really uncomfortable and embarrassed. At that very moment Alison walked into the bar. Barney instinctively pushed Fiona away, which didn't look good.

'Oh, I see. This is all very cosy.'

'It's not what it looks like', protested Barney.

'That's very original. It's not what it looks like. Is that the best you can come up with? How long has this been going on?'

'There's nothing going on.'

'You bastard. I manage to get rid of one horrible husband, and now I find I've got another. No wonder you didn't want me to come. I would have obviously got in your way.'

Fiona intervened, 'I'm so sorry Alison. But I'm in love with him. I always have been. I can't help it.'

'And you can fuck off, you shameless hussy! Find a man of your own.'

There was a brief silence. Barney was dumbstruck. He couldn't believe what was happening. He'd known Fiona for many years. He had no idea this was how she felt. He had always seen her as a friend, and a teammate. She had never given him any suggestion she was romantically interested in him. If only she had. She was an attractive woman with a terrific personality. And a brilliant darts player. It was highly unlikely he would have turned her down. Why has she waited until now? He had been single for years, but now he was married, and his wife thinks he's been having an affair. He just sat in an embarrassed silence, not knowing what to do or say next.

Alison broke the silence. She started laughing.

'I'll tell you what Fiona. Buy me a Bacardi and Coke and you can have him. Throw in a packet of crisps.'

'Nah. I've changed my mind. You can keep him', replied Fiona, bursting out laughing at the same time.

Then there was further laughing from the rest of the gang who were hiding around the corner. Barney realised he'd been taken for a ride.

'You rotten bastards!'

The laughter went on for ages, and Barney felt stupid. Fiona finally offered him an explanation.

'It serves you right. You were correct when you thought you'd offended me when you asked if I had a husband or boyfriend. How many years have you known me? I've never had a husband or boyfriend. Men just don't do it for me. Even you.

They're fine to play darts with, and drink with, but that's about it. I was upset with you for not knowing, and thought you needed to be taught a lesson. And for you information, I do have a partner. A lovely lady called Marie.'

Barney didn't know what to say. He was just going to have to take it on the chin and endure mockery for the rest of the evening. Alison detected his embarrassment and decided it was her wifely duty to comfort him.

'I'm sorry I did that to you. It wasn't my idea.'

'Hmmph.'

'You know I really love you, don't you?'

'Is that you talking , or the Bacardi and coke?'

'It's me talking to the Bacardi and coke.'

This triggered yet more laughter from everybody. Barney had never had to endure such ridicule, and he suspected it wasn't going to stop any time soon.

'You're a real scream tonight.'

'Sorry about that. But you've got to admit we really stitched you up.'

'Yes. You certainly did. But you were a bit too convincing with your verbal assault on me.'

'I know. I was good, wasn't I?'

'It could have backfired?'

'How so?'

'What if I'd accepted Fiona's offer to go back to her room?'

'It wouldn't have happened. She didn't really want you to go.'

'I know that. But what I mean is, just supposing I had said yes to her. What would you have done?'

'Put it this way. Do you remember a lady in the USA back in the nineties called Lorena Bobbit?'

They went out again and had a pub crawl around the town. Barney had to endure more ridicule as the evening went on, and he was getting fed up with it. He asked himself why it mattered that he hadn't been aware of Fiona's sexual orientation. It wasn't something that often cropped up in conversation at darts matches. How could she play such a cruel trick on him? And the part his own wife played. And his friends. He wouldn't forget it. He will have his revenge one day.

When they couldn't find any more open pubs, they all stumbled back for a nightcap and found Eva was just about to close the bar. She allowed them to buy drinks, but then closed up and disappeared. Before she left, she asked them to keep the noise down as there were other guests that would be trying to sleep. They promised they would.

They kept their promise. Most of them. There were some board games in the bar, and they decided to play one. After half an hour Barney told them he was going to bed. He left the others having an intense game of Scrabble. He said goodnight and crept silently towards the staircase. At the bottom of the stairs was a large handbell, the sort used by town criers. He assumed it was used to tell guests it was time for breakfast or dinner. There was even a sign next to it asking people to not touch it.

He disobeyed the sign. He picked up the bell and violently shook it as hard as he could. The noise was horrendous, and the following events even worse. Everyone's initial reaction was to dash out of the room and run upstairs to their rooms. The Scrabble board, and drinks went flying. Alison's drink ended up in Fiona's face. Barney thought there was some justice in that as he sneaked back to his room, just before Eva came out and started shouting at them. The last laugh belonged to him.

Epilogue

Forty Years Later

It was a month after Barney's 90th birthday. He had been looking for a good way to celebrate it, and as luck would have it, Sunderland had made it to the European Champions League final. They were playing against Inter Milan at the Stade de France in Paris. Barney wasn't in the best of health. He was impressed he had managed to make it to ninety, given all the drinking he'd done throughout his life. But it would have taken a lot to stop him being at this game. Sunderland hadn't won a major tournament since the Papa John's trophy way back in 2021. They had won the FA Cup three years ago when they beat Brighton and Hove Albion in the final, but the FA Cup was no longer considered a major trophy. Barney hadn't been able to go to either of those matches. The Papa John's Trophy was played at Wembley without any fans, due to a virus which was threatening the world at the time, and tragically killed millions of conspiracy theorists who refused to get vaccinated. Three years ago, he was too ill to travel to London for the FA Cup final, which was held at the Pot Noodle Stadium, formerly known as Brisbane Road, the home of Leyton Orient FC. Wembley was no longer used for football. It was mainly used these days for American football, reality TV programs, and boy band concerts.

Barney had been helped to get there by his son Jack. Jack was now a fanatical Sunderland supporter. It had taken Barney some time to get him interested in football, but once he was hooked, he was stuck with it forever. His friend Louis also came to Sunderland matches with him, and he was here today too. His parents Liam and Mary were with them in Paris, but didn't come to the game. They preferred to wander around the Louvre, or go up the Eiffel Tower. Liam couldn't remember if he'd been up the Eiffel Tower before. Louis and Jack had extremely short haircuts. They looked like the skinheads who went to football back in the nineteen seventies. It was a fashionable style again, but there was none of the aggro or bovver that skinheads of old were associated with. These days they were the sort of skinheads who helped old ladies to cross the road. Alison had been shocked when Jack first shaved off the blonde, curly hair she was so proud of. It may even have contributed to her second, and fatal heart attack. They had lost her seven years ago. Alison had visited Kenneth in prison, a year into his sentence. She didn't laugh in his face. Nor did she show him any forgiveness. She went along purely for her own benefit. She wanted some kind of closure. It was the first time she had talked to him when she was in control. She noticed he was limping slightly. Her swing of the cricket bat had caused him some sort of permanent damage. She didn't feel sorry for him. It was his own fault. She didn't stay long, and never saw him again. Barney never did get his fuses.

The cats, George and Mildred were also long gone. Alison had buried them at the bottom of the garden and made little headstones for them. Barney got the blame for their deaths, even though he hadn't done anything to contribute to their demise. They died of natural causes, and they were very old. Mildred was still hostile to him right to the very end. They never did get a dog.

Fiona was there with her wife Marie, and Tom was there with

his latest girlfriend Sophie, who was twenty-seven years younger than him. They all thought she was a gold digger, and they were probably right given that every girlfriend he has ever had, had turned out to be a gold digger. Roy had died nine years ago, and Daffy was too frail to travel. It was never going to be the sort of wild partying they used to do in the past. They were all getting old. They would certainly have a few drinks, but nothing like the amount they used to get through. Barney just wanted Sunderland to win, and his life would be complete.

Neil had also managed to get there. He wasn't sitting in the same part of the stadium as the rest of them, but Barney had managed to meet him for a drink earlier. He was very pleased Neil was there. He had fond memories of the times they would meet for a drink in Sunderland before the match, and of the times when they celebrated in style after a victory.

In one of the bars at the stadium, the seven of them had a drink as they waited for the kick off. There was a vending machine in the bar, and as always, Barney made a beeline for it out of curiosity. He was always keen to find how vending machines had developed over the years since he last worked on them. If Liam and Mary had been there, they would have most likely had a look too. But the rest of them understandably weren't interested.

The machine was very different from the ones he used to repair. It recognised the user from their voice, or fingerprints. While he watched, customers asked for products in French, Italian, and English. The machine didn't mind which. The machine also gave health warnings whenever a drink was vended, and predicted the percentage chance of staying healthy, becoming ill, or dying. It didn't stop anyone using it. It then asked the user to agree not to sue the vending company if anything happened to them as a result of using the machine. It also had a television screen which was showing adverts in between people buying stuff. Then just before they were due to kick off, the screen switched to showing the match. They went to take their seats in the stadium.

The game was a huge anti-climax. There were no goals after ninety minutes. The half hour of extra time was slightly better, with both teams scoring a goal. With the game ending up all square, it meant there was going to be the dreaded penalty shootout. By now Barney was desperate to go to the toilet. He wasn't very mobile these days, but hoped he could get to the gents and back before the penalties started. But he was too slow. After he left the toilet, he walked past the vending machine and looked at the screen which was still showing the game. It was already 3-3 in the penalty shootout, so he knew there was no way he could get back to his seat in time to see the outcome. He would have to watch the most momentous sporting occasion of his life on a vending machine.

Barney was feeling dizzy. He thought he could see an alien standing next to him.

'You've picked a bad time to turn up mate. Come back after the game and I'll try to explain about haircuts, getting hit in the balls, and cars that go over a hundred miles an hour. And maybe even why some men think farting is macho.'

'No, Earthling. I'm not interested in any of those things. What I would really like to know is why is it so important to you that Sunderland win this game?'

'That's a tricky question. I don't know the answer. I don't know why, but it just is.'

Then the imaginary vision of the alien disappeared, and Barney turned his attention back to the penalty shootout.

Inter Milan missed their next penalty, but then Sunderland missed too. It was so stressful. Barney didn't know if he could bear watching. He could feel his heart beating far too quickly, and his hands were trembling. Both teams scored their next ones, and at 4-4 after five penalties each, it meant there would be sudden death. Both teams scored again, then Inter Milan missed, meaning Sunderland only had to score to win the Champions League. Barney's nerves were shredded. Could they score? Alas, he would never know. It all got a bit too much for him, and his frail body packed up on him. He was off to the great vending machine in the sky, with an out of order sign pinned to his chest.

That same year there were thirteen people killed by sharks. Ten of those were killed in Shark Bay, Australia. The Australian government had changed the name from Shark Bay to Surfers Paradise in order to encourage tourism, but were forced to change it back again because the tourists kept getting eaten. By contrast Barney was the only person that year to be killed by a vending machine. He always knew it would eventually happen …

Printed in Great Britain
by Amazon

27537062R00126